FANDEMIC

JENNIFER ESTEP

Fandemic

ISBN-13: 978-0-9861885-1-0

Cover Art © 2017 by Jennifer Zemanek/Seedlings Design Studio
Interior Formatting by Author E.M.S.

Fonts: *Playfair Display* by Claus Eggers Sørensen, used under SIL Open Font License, *Baskerville* by Monotype Typography, used under Desktop License, *Type Embellishments One LET* by Esselte Letraset, Ltd., used with permission.

Published in the United States of America

THE BIGTIME SERIES
by Jennifer Estep

Karma Girl

Hot Mama

Jinx

A Karma Girl Christmas (holiday story)

Nightingale

Fandemic

FANDEMIC

by

JENNIFER ESTEP

BOOK FIVE IN THE BIGTIME SERIES

To all the fans of the Bigtime series who wanted more stories,
this one's for you.

To all the fans, never stop enjoying the things that make you happy.

To my mom and my grandma—for everything.

PART ONE

PIPER

CHAPTER ONE

I've always wanted to be a superhero.

Always wanted to have amazing powers. Wear a cool costume. Be dark, brooding, and mysterious. Say wise, knowing, slightly cheesy lines. Use my powers for the greater good and kick some serious ubervillain ass. You know, the whole superhero shtick.

Over the years, I've done everything in my power to make it happen. I've accidentally-on-purpose put my hands next to scary-looking bugs. Gotten a little too close to some of the more unusual animals at the Bigtime Zoo. Taken multiple tours of the Bigtime Nuclear Power Plant. Actually, I still do that last one at least once a year. Just on the off chance that one of the core reactors will melt down and blast me with radiation that gives me superstrength. Or supersenses. Or superanything. I'm not picky.

"Hey, hey, hot mama! Wanna see my sword?"

At the moment, I would have especially loved the power to make myself invisible.

I looked up to find a guy wearing a Striker costume not-so-subtly leering at my breasts the way he had been ever since I'd come over to the bar to get a glass of Wynter punch. He'd finally decided to make his move and get up close and personal about his leering. Oh, goody.

Black hair, brown eyes, bronze skin. The guy was cute, and he had the broad shoulders and muscled body to pull off the skintight leather he was wearing from head to toe. But instead of admiring just how well he filled out certain areas of that leather, I found myself growing annoyed instead.

Because his costume was *all wrong*.

The outline of two small swords that crisscrossed the guy's chest was backwards and red, instead of dark gray like the ones on the *real* Striker's costume. The swords were located above the *F5* insignia, instead of behind it, like they should have been, and the whole suit was a smoky charcoal, instead of a true, midnight black like the one that the real superhero wore.

Amateur.

I might not be a superhero or have any actual superpowers, but I knew more than enough about the heroes and villains in this town to at least get my costume *right*. And I most definitely did not want to get hit on all night long by guys dressed in knockoff Striker suits. But that's exactly what had been happening for the last two hours. I should have expected as much, since I was at the Valentine's Day dance for the *Slaves for Superhero Sex* club.

More than a thousand people had crowded into the Bigtime Convention Center and Orchestra Hall for the annual event, and almost everyone was wearing some sort of colorful costume, mask, cape, or T-shirt emblazoned with the photo and symbol of their favorite hero or villain.

Striker, Fiera, Mr. Sage, Hermit, Karma Girl. All the members of the Fearless Five, the city's preeminent and most popular superhero team, were well represented among the enthusiastic fangirls and fanboys. So were other iconic heroes like Johnny Angel, Debonair, and Talon.

Many folks had also dressed up like their favorite ubervillains, including everyone from Malefica, Frost, and Scorpion from the Terrible Triad to deceased and comatose villains like Prism, Hangman, and Bandit. One woman had suited up like Intelligal and had even built an exact replica of the dead villain's Intellichair, although the woman's chair just rolled on the floor, instead of flying through the air like Intelligal's had. Still, I had to give her props for getting all the details exactly right. It wasn't her fault she hadn't been able to get her hands on a jet-propulsion system to actually make the chair fly.

Even more colorful than the costumes and capes were the decorations that adorned the convention center's main auditorium. Ten-foot-tall cardboard cutouts of heroes and villains towered above the crowd, along with smaller, life-size versions that you could put your arm around and have your picture taken with. Hero- and villain-shaped balloons filled a white netting that swooped down from the ceiling, while still more balloons drifted freely through the air, many of which were in the form of various body parts that I didn't look too closely at. They didn't call the club *Slaves for Superhero Sex* for nothing.

Balloons shaped like giant candy conversation hearts had been tied at either end of the bar, which was set up in the orchestra pit. Several round tables clustered in front of the bar, where people could sit, drink, and talk, as well as play cards and throw dice in the latest role-playing games. Beyond the tables, dozens of couples were grooving on the dance floor, their colorful capes rippling around their spandex-clad bodies. Vendors hawking everything from imitation swords to replica gadgets to collector-edition toys stalked up and down in front of booths that ringed the dance floor, trying to entice people to ignore the pulsing music, come over, and browse through their wares.

I signaled the bartender that I needed a refill, then dug into one of the glass dishes filled with candy conversation hearts that were spaced along the bar. I grabbed a pink heart and read the saying. *I luv superheroes.* Truer words, never spoken. I popped the candy heart into my mouth and crunched down on it.

The bartender finished with my drink and slid a fresh glass of Wynter punch over to me. I reached for the ice-blue concoction, but the guy in the knockoff Striker suit propped his elbow up on the bar in front of my drink and leaned in closer. I didn't need my best friend Abby Appleby's supersense of smell to tell me that he'd taken a bath in his cologne. The overpowering spicy scent made my eyes water and nose twitch in an all-too-familiar way. I was going to have to get rid of him before my allergies kicked into overdrive. A red, runny nose would so not go with the flame-shaped mask that covered my face.

"I'm talking to you, hot mama," the guy crooned again.

"Really?" I asked. "Hot mama? That's your line?"

The guy frowned. "What's wrong with *hot mama?*"

I shrugged. "For starters, it sounds like some cheesy book title."

His frown deepened. "But you're wearing a Fiera costume. Everybody knows that she has fire-based powers." His eyes dropped to my breasts again. "And that she is smokin' hot. Like, *literally.* Just like you are in that costume. Well, without the actual smoke and fire, of course. But you're still plenty hot enough for me in the figurative sense."

Part of me was impressed that he knew the difference between literal and figurative, but the other part of me was growing more and more annoyed by the excessive leering.

I snapped my fingers in front of his face. "Hey, buddy. I'm up here."

He grinned, evidently thinking the snarky finger snap meant that I was totally into him too. "So what do you say, hot mama? Wanna ditch the party and go have a private one of our own?" He waggled his eyebrows for extra emphasis, as though I didn't already know exactly what he meant.

"Sorry." I sniffed and tossed my black hair back over my shoulder in my very best Fiera impersonation. "As you pointed out, I'm dressed like Fiera, and you're in a Striker costume. The two don't mix."

He frowned again. "Why not?"

"You seriously don't know?"

He shook his head.

"Because Karma Girl and Striker are an item. I even think they're married in real life, but that's just a theory of mine."

Actually, it was much more than just a theory, since I'd attended the wedding of Carmen "Karma Girl" Cole and Sam "Striker" Sloane last year. Of course, the two of them didn't realize that I knew who they were, alter egos and all. To them, I was just Piper Perez, a business associate and the chief financial officer of Fiona Fine Fashions. But my inner fangirl had been secretly, gushingly, absolutely *thrilled* to attend the wedding of two of my favorite heroes. After all they'd been through battling the Terrible Triad, Carmen and Sam deserved some happiness, and so did their alter egos.

"Theories?" the guy said, an incredulous note creeping into his voice. "You have *theories* about superheroes?"

And that was the official dagger killing any chance he'd had of picking me up. But the guy kept staring at me like he had no idea what I was talking about, so I listed some more reasons we were never going to happen.

"Of course I have theories about superheroes. Who doesn't? Besides, *everybody* knows that Fiera only goes out with Johnny Angel," I said. "If you were a *true* superhero fan, you'd know that too."

"So what?" the guy asked, staring at my breasts again. "What does it matter who dates who? It's not like we're the real heroes. We're just here to party and have a good time."

I snapped my fingers again. "Eyes up top, buddy. And yeah, maybe we are here to party and have a good time, but I also happen to be a superhero fan. A *true* fan. One who knows her heroes and villains forwards and backwards. Which means that I never, ever go home with guys who don't know their basic facts."

"Are you serious?" the guy asked. "You're turning me down just because I didn't know that some hero chick is dating some villain dude?"

"Two chicks and two dudes, and they're all heroes now," I automatically corrected him. "And that's only one reason. Your overpowering cologne is another one, but your main offense is that sad, sad excuse for a costume. I know that Striker updated his suit a few weeks ago, but still, you had plenty of time to tweak your own suit to match his."

Was I being a total bitch right now? Oh, yeah. Normally, I would have let him down nice and easy, but he was the fifth guy to come up to me in the last hour, and the third one to use the cheesy *hot mama* line. Apparently, some guys thought that wearing an orange-red spandex Fiera costume made you ready, willing, and eager to fulfill all of their warped fantasies for the night, since they'd never get close to the real superhero herself.

The guy sputtered like a car engine, trying to come up with some snappy retort. Evidently, he couldn't believe that I was passing up the opportunity to go back to his place and let him paw me.

I didn't give him the chance to make a comeback. Since his elbow was still blocking my glass of Wynter punch, I grabbed a couple more conversation hearts out of the candy dish, popped them in my mouth, and walked away. Unlike his outfit, *my* costume was one-hundred-percent correct, from my flame-shaped mask to my orange-red catsuit to my chunky-heeled boots—the latter of which helped me make a quick getaway.

I strolled past the boisterous vendors, having already examined their goods and picked up a few new collectibles, and headed for the buffet tables lining one wall. Maybe I was channeling Fiera tonight because I felt like I could eat as much as she did. Okay,

okay, so I couldn't eat a dozen of anything even at my hungriest, but I'd skipped lunch, and I was starving. Watch out, Caveman Stan mini cheeseburgers and Pimpler pepperoni pizza—

I was so focused on the buffet and my growling stomach that I bumped into a tall woman standing off to one side of the tables. Actually, *bumped* wasn't the right word. I hit her shoulder and bounced off, since I was no match for her superstrength, not even when she was standing still.

The woman turned to stare at me. She was wearing an ice-blue suit that brought out the golden sheen of her cropped hair. Silver sequins were stitched together in the shape of a giant snowflake on the front of her costume, and the symbol flashed like a strobe light with every move she made.

I brightened. "Oh, hi, Sabrina. How are you?"

The woman's ice-blue eyes narrowed behind her snowflake-shaped mask, and she crossed her arms over her chest. Too late, I realized my mistake. I'd just called Wynter, the superhero, by her real name—a name I wasn't supposed to know.

But I'd figured out that Sabrina St. John moonlighted as Wynter, the hero who had superstrength and ice-based powers to match her frosty name. Okay, okay, so I hadn't actually figured it out so much as I'd seen her duck into one of the dressing rooms at Oodles o' Stuff, the department store where she worked, and come out thirty seconds later all decked out in her Wynter costume. But I knew who she was all the same. In fact, I knew the real identities of pretty much every hero in Bigtime, and some of the villains too.

Since, you know, most of them had either saved or threatened me at some point over the years.

"I don't know who you think I am, but I'm Wynter—the *real* Wynter." She tapped the sequined snowflake on her chest for emphasis.

"My mistake. Of course you are," I said. "But what are you doing here? Shouldn't you be out patrolling? Keeping the city safe from villains and the like?"

Wynter huffed. "Believe me, I *wish* I was doing that. But it's my turn to chaperone this year's shindig. I can't believe that I let Abby book me for this."

She muttered the last few words under her breath, but I still caught the reference to Abby, who was the city's premiere event planner, in addition to being my best friend. I knew that Abby had planned the Valentine's Day party, but I hadn't realized that she'd gotten Wynter to be one of the guest superheroes. Then again, I hadn't told Abby that I was coming here tonight. Abby loved me, but she thought that I took my hero worship just a little too seriously. Which I totally did. Not that I would ever admit that to her, though.

"I mean, come on," Wynter said. "I know that parts of the auditorium are dark, but they're not *that* dark."

She gestured at a couple standing in a pool of shadows a few feet away from us who were kissing and fondling each other a little too passionately for such a public place.

I winced and turned away from the PDA. The *Slaves for Superhero Sex* club had a bad reputation because some of the members took the club's name far too literally. All right, *way* too literally. Some folks in the club did stupid, foolish, and life-threatening things like stepping out into traffic during rush hour, climbing out onto ledges thirty stories up, or deliberately capsizing their sailboats in the middle of Bigtime Bay. All so they could get a little face time with whichever hero rescued them. Most of the heroes like Wynter politely turned down everything but autograph requests, but there were a few like Gentleman George who enjoyed the, um, *attention* as much as the club members did.

Most people, Abby included, thought the entire *Slaves for Superhero Sex* club was made up of such rabid fans. But really, the Obsessors, as they were called, were a small minority in the group, as were the Villifiers, the people who worshipped villains and tried to get hired on as henchmen and women. Most folks in the club simply loved all things superhero and ubervillain, just like I did. Still, I couldn't judge either faction. At least, not until I gave up my annual nuclear power plant tour.

During the Valentine's Day party, I'd spotted several giggling couples sneaking off to the darker, quieter, more secluded parts of the auditorium to have some alone time with each other. Instead of chasing after heroes and villains, the couples were pretending that they were the real deals tonight, instead of just regular guys and gals dressed in spandex and leather and sporting whips and chains. But I couldn't fault them for that either, given the orange-red fabric that currently clung to my own body like a second skin—

WHOOSH!

A violent wind swept through the auditorium, hard enough to make my black hair fly around my face. The wind gusted again and again, sending all the comic books on the vendors' tables swirling up into the air, rattling the pink candy conversation hearts in their glass dishes, and making the heart balloons attached to the bar whip back and forth like they were caught in the middle of a tornado. It was a tornado, all right—a superhero-fueled one.

The wind died down as suddenly as it had sprung up, and a tall, lean man appeared on the dance floor, right in the middle of all the grooving couples. He wore an opalescent white costume that shimmered with all the colors of the rainbow, along with matching sneakers from Bella Bulluci's latest collection. A pair of wings outlined in silver, his superhero symbol, stretched across his chest, and a wing-shaped mask covered his face, although it didn't even come close to hiding his wide grin.

I recognized him immediately.

Swifte, one of Bigtime's most popular superheroes.

And the guy who'd broken my heart.

Chapter Two

Everyone froze, eyes widening and mouths gaping open at the sudden appearance of the speedy superhero in their midst. The music screeched to a stop, and silence filled the auditorium.

Swifte looked around, then slapped his hands on his hips, stuck his chest out, and lifted his chin, striking the classic, conquering superhero pose. If he'd been wearing a cape, it would have been fluttering dramatically behind him, even though there was no longer any wind inside the auditorium.

When people realized that Swifte—the *real* Swifte—had shown up for the party, all the dancers around him started yelling, cheering, and clapping. Within seconds, so did everyone else in the auditorium, from the partygoers to the vendors to the bartenders.

Everyone except me.

Instead of hooting and hollering, I raised my hand to my chest and rubbed my heart, trying to soothe the sudden ache there, the same terrible ache I felt whenever I saw Swifte, whether it was on the Superhero News Network, racing by on the street, or in person at events like this one.

"Show-off," Wynter muttered, although a fond note of affection warmed her cool voice.

"Yeah," I murmured. "He does love to make a dramatic entrance."

Folks were already clustered three deep around Swifte, holding out their posters, bags, toys, and T-shirts for him to sign, which he was doing at lightning-fast speed, thanks to his superpower. One woman forced her way to the front of the crowd and shoved a filmy bit of pink lace right into his face.

"Swifte! Swifte! You have to sign my bra!" The woman stopped yelling and batted her lashes at him. "Along with anything else you'd like."

My hand dropped from my heart like a lead weight and balled into a tight fist.

Wynter noticed the motions, along with the anger pinching my lips. "Uh-oh. Don't be jealous and go all Yeti Girl on me."

"I'm not jealous," I muttered, even though I totally was.

"*Right.*" She drawled out the word. "And Hot Stuff and I get along like peanut butter and chocolate."

"Sure. If peanut butter and chocolate were archenemies who wanted nothing more than to destroy each other."

Wynter shrugged. "Just trying to cheer you up, Piper."

She winced as soon as the last word left her mouth. Too late, she realized her mistake—that she'd called me by *my* real name, something she wasn't supposed to know if we were complete strangers like she'd claimed earlier.

"Snowballs," she cursed.

But I was too busy staring at Swifte to care about Wynter's slipup. He finished signing the woman's bra and handed it back to her. But before he could turn to autograph the next person's bag, the woman looped her bra around his neck, pulled him up next to her, and planted her lips on his.

More hoots and hollers rose up, along with catcalls and several loud *atta-girls!* You would think that a superspeedy superhero like Swifte could easily duck out of a surprise lip lock, but he made no move to disengage himself from the woman.

Disgusted, I turned away from them. I wasn't hungry. Not anymore. Not even for Caveman Stan mini cheeseburgers. All I wanted to do right now was get away from the stomach-churning sight of Swifte kissing another woman.

Still, I took a moment to be polite to Wynter. "Thanks for coming to the dance. I'm sure all the club members appreciate it. I'll get your autograph next time. See you later."

I stomped past the buffet tables, my gaze fixed on the exit doors at the back of the auditorium. Maybe if I was lucky, Swifte would be so busy smooching his adoring fan that he wouldn't even realize I had been here and had seen the whole thing—

"The spotlight!" someone yelled. "Watch out! It's going to fall!"

I cringed and looked up, dreading but already knowing exactly what I would find. Sure enough, I stood directly below said spotlight, which was dangling by a single thin wire, one that was sparking, cracking, and flashing a sinister blue-white with electricity. Even as my gaze locked on to the spotlight, the wire snapped free from the ceiling, and the heavy metal contraption started to fall—zooming toward me at warp speed.

Abby always joked that I was in the wrong place at the right time, but her words were all too true. I didn't have luck as a superpower, not like Bella Bulluci did, but I must have been born under an unlucky star to get into as much trouble as I did. For some reason, I was *always* around when bad things happened. If the Skyline Bridge collapsed, my car would be the one right in the middle of the span. If a freak storm surged up out of Bigtime Bay, I'd be the one fishing out on the end of the pier. If a fire started in Tip-Top Tower, I'd be the one trapped in an elevator on the highest floor.

And it wasn't like I put myself into these situations on purpose. Not like the Obsessors did. They just happened to me, over and over and over again. I must have done something truly horrible in another life to be put into so much danger in this one. Or maybe my karma was just that bad.

I would have been perfectly happy developing superpowers and rescuing myself from all these dangerous situations. Or just calling the Fearless Five hotline for help or even good, old-fashioned 911. But instead, it seemed like every time I got into trouble, there was always a hero waiting to rescue me. Granny Cane, Grandpa Pain, Debonair, Black Samba. Even Lulu Lo had saved me once by pushing me out of the way of a runaway horse carriage in Paradise Park, and she wasn't even an official hero. Although she was engaged to one, since she and Henry "Hermit" Harris were getting married soon, another event that Abby was planning.

Maybe I really had been born under a lucky star, instead of an unlucky one, since I kept getting rescued by all these heroes. At least being in so many bad situations made it easier to get their autographs to add to my collection.

Those were the odd, jumbled, nonsensical thoughts that raced through my mind as I watched the spotlight fall. My brain finally kicked into gear and told my legs to *move-move-move*, but even as I surged forward, trying to get out of the way, I knew that I was going to be too slow to escape the death that was dropping down right on top of my head—

At the very last second, just before the spotlight would have turned me into Pancake Piper, a body slammed into mine and knocked us both forward and out of the way.

BOOM!

For several seconds, there was just noise. The loud, jarring, echoing *crash-crash-crash* of the spotlight hitting the auditorium floor, then smashing, snapping, and splintering into a thousand pieces. The *crunch-crunch* of metal tearing apart, the *tinkle-tinkle* of glass breaking, and the *squeal-squeal-squeal* of screws ripping loose. But through it all, that warm, strong, lean body covered my own, shielding me from the fallout.

The destructive noises finally stopped, although they were quickly replaced by hurried footsteps, concerned whispers, and louder and louder shouts for someone to get some help in here already.

I opened my eyes to find Swifte staring down at me, his light blue gaze locking with my dark brown one.

"Are you okay?" he asked in a low, husky tone that always sent shivers down my spine, even now, when we were the center of attention.

"Yeah," I replied, my voice hoarse with all sorts of emotions that I wanted to keep hidden from everyone, but especially him.

I hesitated, then reached up and brushed some bits of glass out of his sandy-brown hair. Swifte's eyes softened, and he cupped my cheek. I turned into his touch, feeling the warmth of his skin, even through his white, opalescent glove.

"Move, move, move! Official superhero chaperone coming through!" Wynter's voice thundered out, and she dropped to her knees beside us. "Are you guys okay?"

I jerked my face away, and Swifte dropped his hand and hissed out a breath. The next instant, he was back on his feet. He leaned down and held out his hand in normal speed. I sighed, then took it, and he slowly, gently, carefully pulled me up onto my own feet.

"Are you okay?" Swifte repeated the question.

I gave him a thin, brittle smile. "I'm fine. I'm always fine. You know that. Thanks for the rescue…again."

Swifte gave me a short, curt nod, not quite looking at me the same way I was not quite looking at him. Wynter's gaze snapped back and forth between the two of us, picking up on the weird, tense vibe. But when she realized that we were both fine and that neither one of us was going to look at or talk to the other, she faced the crowd and started shooing away the gawkers.

"All right, folks," Wynter called out. "Show's over. As you were. Except for you two over there by the buffet tables. This is a party, not a hotel. Go get a room if you want to do that sort of thing. What? What did you say? No, I do not want to join you for a threesome!"

Wynter kept arguing with the enthusiastic couple, and the crowd slowly dispersed. The music cranked back up into high gear, and a minute later, everyone was eating, talking, drinking, dancing, and partying just as hard as they had been before.

But Swifte stayed where he was in front of me. He drew in a breath and opened his mouth like he was going to say something. I sucked in a breath too, my treacherous, traitorous heart rising with hope and anticipation—

"Oh! Oh, my! That was *so* heroic!" The woman with the lacy pink bra was back, wiggling in between us.

Swifte tried to look past her at me, but she kept moving from side to side, blocking his view. I didn't know what he'd been about to say, but it didn't matter. It wouldn't have changed anything between us. Nothing I had said had kept him from breaking up with me all those months ago. Bitter much, Piper? Oh, yeah.

So I left Swifte to deal with his adoring fan and hurried out of the auditorium, once again wishing that I had a superpower.

Because now was one of those times when the ability to disappear would have definitely come in handy.

Sick of all things Swifte and superhero-related, I left the auditorium, stripped off my flame-shaped Fiera mask, and retrieved my coat and bag of collectibles from the checkroom.

I shrugged into the gray wool and pulled on my matching fleece gloves. The coat ruined the sleek look of my Fiera costume, but I didn't care. Hearts might be warm with love, romance, and other ooey-gooey sentiments on Valentine's Day, but February was still one of the coldest months in Bigtime, and I wasn't walking home in paper-thin spandex when it was only five degrees outside. Too bad I wasn't really Fiera. Then I could have just used my own fire powers to keep me warm.

I headed toward the exit doors, waving to Eddie Edgars, the college-age security guard who worked the front desk at the convention center during many of the events. Eddie gave me a short, distracted wave and flipped another page in his comic book. Curious, I changed direction and walked over to see what he was reading. Eddie was a fanboy himself, and he'd gotten into the spirit of tonight's event. Instead of his usual guard uniform, he sported a green-and-white outfit with a flowing cape in honor of Mr. Sage, the Fearless Five member with psychic powers.

"Hi, Eddie."

"Hey, Piper." His gaze flicked over me. "Great costume, from what I can see of it. Really authentic."

"Thanks. Yours too. What are you reading?"

Eddie showed me the cover, which featured Talon standing on top of a building in all his cobalt-blue, leather-clad glory, holding up his crossbow gun as though he were going to shoot a bolt straight into the moon.

"It's the latest Talon story by Confidante," Eddie said. "The one about him taking out Bandit and Tycoon a few weeks ago."

Confidante was another one of Bigtime's heroes, one who was sort of like a gossip monger for the hero-villain set. She churned out comic book after comic book chronicling the latest adventures of the city's heroes and villains, including the Fearless Five, Debonair, Wynter, and others. Somehow, she got all the inside scoop on all the heroes' and villains' fights and feuds—despite the fact that no one even knew what she looked like, much less who she actually was. Even I didn't have a clue as to Confidante's real identity.

"That's a really good issue. *So* much better than her recent Swifte series."

Eddie blinked. "You didn't like the Swifte series? But I thought you were his number-one fan."

"Not anymore," I muttered, trying to ignore the ache in my heart.

Eddie gave me another strange look, so I plastered a smile on my face.

"Anyway, I should be going. Early day tomorrow and all that."

"Good night, Piper."

"Good night, Eddie."

I left his desk, walked over to the revolving doors, and stepped outside. The winter air slapped me in the face, even colder than I'd expected, and I turned up the collar of my coat and tucked my chin down inside it as far as I could. My phone beeped, and I pulled it out of my pocket to check the message.

I *finally* got her on the plane. Turning off our phones now. Take care of Rascal for us. See you in a week. W.

I grinned. Looked like Wesley "Talon" Weston had made good on his secret plan to whisk Abby away for a much-needed vacation, since she'd been working twelve-hour days for the past few weeks, trying to get everything ready for the *SSS* dance and all the other Valentine's Day dinners, engagement parties, and weddings she'd been planning. Good. My perfectionist friend needed the vacation, and it was going to be a great one. Wesley was flying them on his private plane to Cloudburst Falls to take in the sights there before they drove down to Ashland and then headed over to Cypress Mountain to do some skiing.

Tell Abby not to worry. Going to get Rascal right now. Have fun! XOXO. P.

I sent the message to both of them and waited for a response, but there wasn't one, so I slid my phone into my pocket and pulled my gloves back onto my hands. Abby would probably call or text me tomorrow. Wesley might get her to turn off her phone for the rest of the night, but Abby would crack sooner or later and check her messages, if only to make sure that Rascal was okay and that there were no crises at *A+ Events*, her event-planning business.

I was happy for my best friend, and I was so glad that she had such a great guy like Wesley in her life. Someone who was kind and thoughtful and totally in love with her. But it also made me feel a little sad, lonely, and depressed. Because I'd had a guy like that in my life too.

And I'd gone and screwed it all up.

The winter wind whistled down the street, reminding me yet again how cold it was and what a sad, sad cliché I was turning out to be, standing by myself and moping in the night. So I headed for Abby's loft, which wasn't far from the convention center.

It had started snowing while I'd been at the *SSS* dance, and the fat, white flakes had already covered the sidewalks and softened the harsh edges of the buildings. I breathed in, enjoying the cold, crisp air after all the perfumes and colognes at the party. It was after midnight now, and technically not Valentine's Day anymore, although strings of white, pink, and red lights glowed in many of the storefronts I passed. But the romantic colors and elaborate displays of white lace, pink hearts, and red roses did absolutely nothing to improve my decidedly blue mood, so I hurried on.

I had just stepped onto Abby's block when a particularly strong gust of wind whipped against my back, spraying snow in every direction. I sighed, knowing what I'd find when I finally managed to shove my hair back out of my face and blink away the icy flakes that had stuck to my eyelashes.

Sure enough, Swifte was standing right in front of me.

The superhero looked around, but the block was dark, except for a few lights that burned in the large brownstone across the street. The one that belonged to Jasper, one of Bigtime's more intriguing and mysterious figures.

When he was satisfied that we were alone, Swifte reached up and took off his wing-shaped mask, revealing sandy-brown hair, blue eyes, and a handsome face that made my heart race even now.

Kyle Quicke stared back at me.

CHAPTER THREE

"Piper."

"Kyle."

And that was all we said to each other.

Then again, maybe that was for the best, since words were what had come between us in the first place. My stupid, stupid words, combined with my not-so-subtle hints about Swifte.

"Are you okay?" Kyle finally asked. "I hope I didn't hurt you when I pushed you out of the way of that spotlight."

I shrugged. "I'm fine. I'm always fine, remember?"

He grimaced. We'd dated for a year, so he was well acquainted with my propensity for being in the wrong place at the right time.

Our relationship had started out small, the way these things so often do. I was at Quicke's, his restaurant, ordering lunch for myself and Fiona, the way I did almost every day, and Kyle and I had started talking, for once going beyond the polite small talk we usually exchanged. He'd grinned at all my cheesy jokes, and he'd made me laugh in return with some of his own. The next day, he was waiting to take my lunch order instead of Ray, the usual waiter. And the day after that...and the day after that... Eventually, Kyle had asked me out, and I'd enthusiastically said yes.

We'd hit it off. We liked the same movies, the same books, even some of the same music. He was kind and thoughtful and went out of his way to do small, sweet things for me, like be waiting outside my office in the morning with a cup of hot chocolate and a dozen doughnuts from Bryn's Bakery. I appreciated the gesture, even if Fiona Fine, my boss, always ate all the doughnuts before I could get my hands on a single one.

But most important of all, Kyle was the first person who'd ever really accepted my love for superheroes and didn't think that I was silly or stupid or that all my collectibles were just a big, fat waste of money. He had understood that I loved a good hero-villain battle as much as the next fangirl, but that I also appreciated what the heroes stood for, how they kept fighting no matter how terrible the odds were stacked against them, and most especially the hope that they gave to all of us that we could be more than we ever thought possible. That we could help other people. That we could actually make a difference in someone's life when it mattered most.

Kyle might be a bona fide superhero himself, but he was still just as big a fan of heroes in general as I was, reading the same comics that I did, going to the same conventions and events, and even arguing with me about which hero had the coolest and most useful power. His appreciation, admiration, and respect for his fellow heroes—and even the villains—were just some of the things that I loved about him.

We'd been so happy, and I had thought for sure that we would be getting engaged and moving in together soon—right up until the day that Swifte had saved me from being run over by a city bus.

I'd been in the crosswalk outside Fiona Fine Fashions when the bus driver had suffered a heart attack and lost control of his vehicle. I'd heard the tires *screech-screech-screech* and had looked up to realize that I was about to be run over. But Swifte had saved me, just like he had tonight at the auditorium. One second, the bus was careening straight toward me. The next, I was standing on the opposite sidewalk, safe and clear of the bus, which had crashed into a streetlight and finally stopped.

Nothing new there, but Swifte's reaction was quite shocking. He'd hugged me tight and given me a deep, passionate kiss before he remembered that he was in costume and wasn't supposed to know me at all. He had zoomed away without a word, but I'd known his kiss, his lips, his touch. In that instant, I'd realized that Swifte was really Kyle.

And I'd been happier than ever before.

I already loved Kyle, but finding out that he was Swifte had been the cherry on top of the awesomesauce sundae that was already him. So when I'd met him for our date that night, I not-so-casually mentioned how the superhero had saved me and how terrific I thought he was. But Kyle didn't say anything back, and he especially didn't confess his secret identity to me the way that I wanted him to.

So I tried again the next day…and the day after that…and the day after that…

I talked about Swifte nonstop over the next week, and I bought all the Swifte-themed merchandise I could get my hands on, plastering it all over my apartment. I did it all as a way to get Kyle to open up, to get him to tell me his secret identity.

But it had all horribly backfired.

Kyle had come over to my apartment for dinner to celebrate our one-year anniversary. But instead of sitting down to his favorite steak-and-potatoes meal that I'd cooked, he'd broken up with me, saying that we just weren't right for each other.

I'd been so surprised and devastated that I hadn't even been able to speak for the better part of a minute. He had his hand on the doorknob to walk out when I'd finally found my voice again and blurted out the truth.

Even now, all these months later, the memory rose up in my mind, as sharp and clear and painful as ever...

"I know that you're really Swifte."

Kyle whipped around, his blue eyes wide with shock. "How did you..."

"You kissed me. I would know your kiss, your touch anywhere." I grinned. "Even if I don't actually have supersenses. That's what I've been trying to tell you by talking about Swifte so much over these past few days. By buying all his, er, your merchandise. That I was okay with it. More than okay with it. I love that you're secretly a superhero. So if that's why you're breaking up with me, don't...don't throw away what we have over something like this."

I stepped forward to take him into my arms, but he backed up against the door, hurt and sadness flashing in his eyes, along with more than a little fear. The last emotion confused me. Why would Kyle be scared of me? He was the one with the superpower, not me.

"And that's exactly why I have to end things, why I have to end this.*"*

I frowned. "Why? I don't understand. I'm crazy about you. I love you, *every part of you, including your alter ago."*

He sighed. "You say that now, but I've been down this road before. More times than I care to remember, actually. Several people have found out about my secret identity over the years. Friends, girlfriends, and other folks. And it never, ever *ends well. They either get obsessed with my being a superhero until Kyle Quicke just fades away and all they want to talk about, all they care about is my being Swifte. Or they get upset at how much time I spend being Swifte and want me to give up being a hero altogether. Eventually, things get so bad that I have to ask Mr. Sage to mindwipe them and erase all their memories and knowledge of my being Swifte."*

"But I would never do either one of those things. You know that. You know me.*"*

He sighed again and shook his head, more hurt filling his face. "You're right. I do know you, Piper. *You might love me, but you love superheroes more than anything else. Even me. And that...well, that's something I just can't live with. I can't go through all of that. Not again. Not even for you. I'm sorry."*

Kyle had given me a sad, knowing smile, then opened the door and left my apartment.

Of course, I had chased after him, but by the time I yanked the door open and stepped out into the hallway, he was long gone. For the first time, I wished that he didn't have any powers—and that I could take back every stupid thing I'd said and done over the past week.

But I couldn't.

Of course, I tried to talk to Kyle after that, tried to explain that I loved him, and not just because he moonlighted as Swifte, but nothing I said changed his mind. I talked and talked and talked until I was as blue in the face as Yeti Girl, but nothing I said convinced him that I was telling the truth. That I wasn't just some rabid *SSS* fangirl who wanted to make time with a hero. That I loved him for, well, *him*.

But Kyle didn't believe me, and he completely tuned me out. Eventually, he had stopped listening to me altogether and had started avoiding me every time our paths crossed. At Quicke's. Charity events. Even when we passed each other on the street, whether he was in costume as Swifte or not.

All the while, I kept expecting Mr. Sage to pop up at my office or outside my apartment building, ready to lay the whammy on me and make me forget all about Kyle being Swifte. But it didn't happen. I'd seen the psychic superhero plenty of times since my breakup with Kyle, but Mr. Sage had never done more than give me a friendly wave. I didn't know why Kyle didn't tell the other superhero to mindwipe me like all the other people who'd found out his secret identity as Swifte.

Either way, Kyle's disbelief, his avoidance, his rejection *hurt*—more than anything else had ever hurt before. It hurt so much that I couldn't even talk to him without wanting to cry and scream and kiss him all at the same time. It hurt so much that I'd started avoiding him the same way that he was me.

It hurt so much that I'd given up trying to change his mind.

Some wannabe superhero I was. A couple months of the silent treatment and cold shoulder and I'd lost hope and stopped fighting for him, stopped fighting for *us*.

But seeing Kyle standing in front of me dressed as Swifte, but with his mask off, just reminded me how happy we'd been together and how I would never find anybody else like him. The guy who'd made me smile and laugh and who'd showed me every single day just how much he'd loved me.

New determination surged through me, overcoming the hollow ache in my heart. Determination to win him back, to get him to really listen to me, and to finally convince him once and for all how much I loved *him*—every single part of him. Real heroes never gave up, and I wasn't going to either. Not anymore.

So I shook off my hurt and inertia and opened my mouth, ready to tell him once again how much I cared for him, whether he was wearing shimmering white spandex or not. "Kyle, I—"

"I just wanted to make sure you were okay," he said, cutting me off. "I'm glad you are, Piper. It's late. I should let you go on home now."

His voice got faster and faster with every single word. He slapped his mask back on, pivoted on his foot, and started to zoom away. I realized that I was about to lose my chance, so I stepped up and blurted out the first thing that popped into my mind.

"I wish things were different," I said. "Between us."

Kyle, Swifte, stopped, every muscle in his body tense and rigid, as though Frost had used his infamous freezoray gun to ice him in place. After a moment, he let out a long, sad sigh. "Yeah. Me too."

"We can make it different. Just give me another chance—" I spit out the words as fast as I could, but I was too slow.

WHOOSH!

The wind whipped up, and more snow swirled against my face. I blinked, but he was already gone.

CHAPTER FOUR

I stood there, waiting, hoping, wishing, but Kyle "Swifte" Quicke didn't zoom back around. And he wouldn't, unless another runaway bus came out of nowhere to mow me down. I looked up and down the dark, snowy street. No buses in sight. Which meant that Swifte was gone, and my heart was still broken, shattered into more tiny, jagged pieces than the fallen spotlight at the auditorium.

"Snowballs," I muttered, echoing Wynter's curse from earlier tonight.

I sighed, my heart heavier and hurting more than ever before, and used my key to let myself into Abby's building and then her loft. As soon as I opened the loft door, a squirming ball of fur hurtled across the room and pounced on my feet, licking the bits of snow off my boots.

I laughed, bent down, and picked up Rascal, the Pembroke Welsh corgi that Abby had adopted a few weeks ago. Like all puppies, Rascal was as cute as cute could be, with sandy-brown fur that covered his back and a chubby white belly that he was more than happy to let anyone rub as long they wanted to. His liquid brown eyes could melt any heart, and even his triangular ears were adorable, even though they were still a little too large for his head.

"Oof!" I said, hefting the puppy up in my arms. "What is Abby feeding you? You're getting so heavy."

Rascal let out a loud, happy bark and licked my cheek. I laughed again, then turned my head and sneezed as my allergies kicked in. I sighed. I really wished that I could go longer than thirty minutes without sneezing violently at something, whether it was pets, pollen, or pollution. But absolutely *everything* made my allergies flare up. Seriously, if there was only a single blade of grass in the entire city, then I would be the person to sneeze at it, even if it was clear on the other side of Bigtime and buried under the snow that was slowly accumulating outside.

That was another reason I wanted some sort of power. Superheroes didn't have *allergies*. Toxic poisons, radioactive formulas, chemical cocktails that could enhance or take away their powers, drive them crazy, or kill them outright. Sure, that was par for the course in Bigtime. But no hero or villain worth his or her spandex was afflicted with something so mundane, so ordinary, and so exceptionally boring as *allergies*.

Then again, I was no hero. Just another fangirl. Kyle used to joke and call me a fandemic, saying that I knew more about heroes and villains than anyone else. Like a scholarly academic of all things super-related. Abby had a slightly less flattering take on the word, claiming that my super-obsession was more like an epidemic of obsessive fangirling. Either way, I didn't mind the nickname too much.

Fandemic. Hmm. Maybe that should be my superhero name, if I ever did miraculously develop powers. Although it would be just my luck to get some lame-ass power, like the ability to make people slightly feverish or something else silly and useless. Heh.

Rascal barked again, so I put him down while I went around the loft, gathering up his food, leash, and chew toys, including a white plush one shaped like Swifte that was among the most mangled. Maybe it was petty, but the sight cheered me up.

I loved Kyle, really, I did, but I also thought that he'd been stupid to dump me. He was a great guy, sure, but I was pretty awesome myself. The kind of sweet, thoughtful significant other who brought him dinner after he'd been working all day at Quicke's so that he wouldn't have to cook something for himself. Who always made sure to have his favorite kinds of food in my fridge. Who brought him books and candy and other small treats just because I knew that he liked them and wanted to brighten his day.

Rascal barked, chomped down on the Swifte toy, yanked it out of my hand, and started wrestling with it, growling all the while.

"Good boy," I said, leaning down to pet Rascal again.

It took me longer than it should have to grab Rascal's gear, since I had to pick my way around more than two dozen cardboard boxes strewn all over the loft. The tops on all the boxes were open, revealing stacks and stacks of vinyl records and CDs inside, along with some old cassette tapes and even a few eight-tracks. The ubervillain Bandit had ransacked Abby's loft a few weeks ago, destroying her music collection, and Abby had been ordering replacement records and CDs like mad ever since. And she thought that I was bad with my superhero collectibles. Please. Pot, meet kettle.

My nose scrunched up with disgust at the enormous mess, and my fingers literally itched to unpack all the boxes, or at least arrange them in some kind of order. I was a total neat freak that way. But Abby would kill me if I touched her music collection, so I resisted the urge to straighten it up, along with the rest of the loft. Abby might be great at planning birthdays, weddings, and SSS parties down to the smallest detail, but she wasn't nearly as organized in her own personal space.

By the time I found Rascal's collar and leash stuffed down behind one of the couch cushions, the puppy was waiting at the door, barking and dancing around like he needed to go outside and do his business.

"Okay, okay," I said. "I'm coming, boy. Just hold on a minute."

I bent down, slipped Rascal's collar over his head, and clipped his leash to it. Both the collar and the leash were cobalt-blue and printed with tiny figures of Talon holding his crossbow gun. Abby had groaned when I'd given them to her last week, but I figured that Rascal should wear his hero's colors proudly.

I looped one end of the leash around my wrist, then grabbed the reusable cloth bag that I'd filled with Rascal's food and toys. It too was cobalt-blue and emblazoned with Talon's bird-and-wings logo. Another present from me to Abby.

Rascal strained toward the door, but I looked back out over the loft, making sure that I hadn't forgotten anything. My gaze landed on the Swifte chew toy, which Rascal had dropped a few feet from the door. I hesitated, then picked it up and placed it into the bag with the rest of the puppy's stuff. Maybe if Rascal grew tired of it, I could get Black Samba to show me how to use it as a voodoo doll and stab some sense into Kyle, one pin at a time. Yeah, it was silly, but the thought made me smile, just a little.

Rascal barked again, so I turned off the lights, led him outside, and locked the loft door behind us.

Rascal and I rode the elevator down to the ground floor, then stepped back out onto the street. It was even colder than before, but the gusting wind and blowing snow didn't seem to bother Rascal at all. The puppy let out another excited, happy bark, then started bounding along, as though he were trying to hop from one pile of snow on the sidewalk to the next. Despite his short, stubby legs, it was all I could do to keep up with him.

Like all puppies, Rascal seemed to have a limitless amount of energy, but his had been augmented since he'd been exposed to euphoridon, a highly addictive drug. Think crack, but with radiation. Abby and Wesley were monitoring the puppy closely to see if he developed any superpowers from the drug, but so far, he seemed to be mostly normal. Except for the whole *bouncing-around-like-a-pint-size-kangaroo* thing.

"If you don't slow down, you're going to dislocate my shoulder with all that hopping," I said.

Rascal immediately stopped his relentless bounding and gave me an apologetic look. Corgis were an intelligent breed, but it already seemed like the euphoridon had made him smarter than most dogs.

I loved Rascal, but I couldn't help but sigh all the same. Because even the puppy had superpowers, and I had nothing but a broken heart.

Across the street, a door opened on the very nice brownstone that took up that block, and a man wearing thick gray coveralls and silver glasses stepped outside. Rascal barked and strained in that direction, pulling me along, despite his small size, so I gave in and crossed the street, following the puppy's lead.

"Hey, Jasper," I called out.

"Hey, Piper."

He waved me over, and I climbed to the top of the brownstone's steps. Rascal barked and started licking Jasper's boots the same way he had mine. Jasper grinned, squatted down, and rubbed the puppy's oversize ears. Rascal grunted with happiness, then flopped down and rolled over, so that Jasper could rub his white belly too.

"Where's Abby?" Jasper asked.

"She's on vacation with Wesley this week, so I'm watching Rascal for them."

Jasper nodded. "Good for them for getting away from the city for a while."

He petted Rascal for another minute before getting to his feet. Jasper tipped his head back and drew in a deep breath of air.

He noticed me watching him and shrugged. "It can get a little stuffy inside sometimes."

"Oh," I said in a bright voice. "Have you been down in your workshop? Are you testing out a new explosive? Something more powerful than explodium?"

Jasper was Bigtime's resident bomb expert. If you wanted to blow something up in loud, spectacular fashion, then Jasper was the guy you called. Even superheroes like Karma Girl and Fiera used his products from time to time, when they needed a little more firepower or wanted a particularly big *BOOM*.

Jasper peered at me through his glasses, then tilted his head to the side, making the small diamond stud twinkle in his ear. "And why would you think something like that?"

Too late I realized that I wasn't supposed to know what Jasper did in his spare time any more than I was supposed to know Wynter's real identity. Normally, I would have done the same *oops-my-mistake* song and dance that I'd done with Wynter earlier tonight, made some lame excuse, and hurried off. But it was late, and I was tired, especially of pretending that I didn't know who was really who in this city.

I laughed. "Jasper, everyone knows about the crazy things you cook up in your brownstone basement. It's, like, the worst-kept secret in all of Bigtime."

He stared at me, his lips pinching together in displeasure.

But it was too late to pretend ignorance now, so I kept on charging straight ahead. "And I've heard certain people talk about you and all the bombs you supply to the Fearless Five and other heroes."

Fiona Fine and Lulu Lo had had a rather interesting discussion about him just last week, when Lulu had come by the Fiona Fine Fashions office to update our computers and networks. Apparently, Fiona was finishing up some clothes she'd promised to design for Jasper in payment for several bombs that he'd supplied to her when she'd gone up against Siren and Intelligal last year.

His pale violet eyes narrowed behind his glasses. "What people?"

Telling him about Fiona would blow her cover as Fiera, so I shrugged. "Just people. Nobody in particular. You know how it is."

Jasper crossed his arms over his chest, and it suddenly occurred to me that chatting him up about his highly illegal bomb-making business wasn't exactly the smartest thing to do. Sometimes, my inner fandemic got the best of me in situations like this. Okay, okay, so in most situations, actually.

"But don't worry. I think that it's supercool that you help out all the heroes. I'm not going to tell anyone about you. I promise." I crossed my finger over my heart, making the proverbial X.

Jasper's lips flattened into a thin line. He petted Rascal again, then gave me a curt nod and disappeared back inside his brownstone. I winced at the loud *bang* of the door slamming shut behind him and several locks *click-click-clicking* home one after another. I'd definitely worn out my welcome here. Piper Perez strikes again.

Rascal whined, wondering why Jasper had gone back inside. I sighed and gently tugged on his leash.

"Come on, boy," I said. "Let's go home before my big mouth gets us into any more trouble tonight."

I led Rascal down the brownstone steps and back out onto the sidewalk, where the puppy finally did his business for the night. It was getting colder, and the snow was falling faster by the minute, so I picked him up and hurried toward my own apartment building.

Rascal let me carry him for three whole blocks before he started squirming. The puppy was heavier than he looked, so I put him down, making sure to keep a firm grip on his leash. Abby would never forgive me if I let anything happen to him, and it would be just my luck to put us both in mortal danger, simply by strolling down the sidewalk and having a subway grate suddenly collapse beneath my feet for no apparent reason, other than my bad karma.

The snow kept falling, and what little traffic there was on the streets died down, until Rascal and I were the only ones outside. Looked like all the heroes and villains had taken the night off for Valentine's Day, just like everyone else. I snorted. Well, I hoped everyone had more luck with their love life tonight than I'd had with mine these past few months.

Rascal and I crossed the street and stepped onto the block that housed Fiona Fine Fashions. The giant marble F that marked the entrance to the store was outlined in neon lights that glowed orange-red, just like Fiona did whenever she used her fire powers as Fiera. Normally, I would have stopped to admire the impressive sign, but I tucked my chin down into the collar of my coat and hurried on.

No cars cruised by on the street outside the *FFF* shop, but a lone vehicle was sitting at the corner curb—a battered old ice cream truck. Weird. I would think that it would be far too late and cold to sell ice cream tonight. Then again, Fiona had ordered three dozen double-chocolate-chip ice cream cakes from Quicke's earlier this week, so what did I know? Still, this truck looked more decrepit than most, and I could barely make out the faded blue words on the dull gray paint. Snowdom Ice Cream Factory. Probably a castoff vehicle someone had gotten on the cheap, since the factory had been closed for a long time now.

I walked by the truck and was passing the alley that ran

beside the store when Rascal stopped. The puppy froze for a moment, then plopped down on his butt in the snow and started looking around, cocking his head first one way, then the other, as though he were using his oversize ears to hear something that no one else could.

I stopped and listened too, but I didn't hear anything. Then again, I didn't have a dog's ears, much less this superpup's even sharper ones. "Come on, Rascal. Whatever you hear, it's too cold to go chasing after it tonight."

I tugged on his leash, but Rascal was heavier and stronger than he looked because I couldn't budge him, and I didn't have the heart to really try. I bent down to scoop him up in my arms again, but he let out a worried bark, then scampered toward the alley entrance with the sudden speed of a rocket. I had no choice but to follow him or get my shoulder dislocated.

Rascal pulled and pulled me along, going deeper and deeper into the alley. I looked left and right, but the only things back here were trash cans filled with colorful scraps of fabric from *FFF* and garbage from all the other nearby stores.

"See?" I said. "There's nothing back here."

But Rascal stuck his black nose down next to the snow-covered asphalt, sniffing and sniffing as if determined to prove me wrong. The end of the alley was bricked up, so I let go of his leash and let him wander off, thinking that maybe he needed to do one final bit of business for the night.

Rascal moved farther back into the alley, and I used the opportunity to pull out my phone and check my messages. But Wesley really must have gotten Abby to turn off her phone because neither one of them had texted me.

I was about to put my phone away when I noticed the glow from the screen was making something shimmer on the alley floor. I angled the phone in that direction, using it as a flashlight, then bent down so I could get a better look at the shimmering object.

A piece of fabric lay on the asphalt.

Given the snow and shadows, I couldn't really tell its exact color, but it seemed to be ice-blue, although there was a darker stain around the edges. I frowned and picked up the fabric, staring at the stain.

Was that…blood?

Rascal let out a sharp, worried bark, then another one, then another one. He also started dancing around, almost like there was something back there he wanted me to come see for myself.

I tucked the fabric into my coat pocket, then got to my feet and hurried over to him. "What is it, boy?"

Rascal skipped to the very back of the alley, where there was a gap between one of the Dumpsters and the brick wall.

A man was sitting in the empty space.

The guy was obviously homeless, given the dirt and grime that covered the layers and layers of clothes he wore and the blue toboggan pulled down low on his forehead. Still, despite the dirt, all his garments were high-end and made out of colorful, expensive fabrics, including a royal-blue-plaid coat that Fiona had sewn herself. She'd given it to him two weeks ago, and he'd been wearing it ever since, along with some matching, fingerless gloves.

I relaxed when I spotted the coat because I knew the guy it belonged to—Bustling Blue, a former ubervillain.

Bustling Blue used to be a minor bad guy in Bigtime some twenty years ago, robbing banks and jewelry stores, then using his speed to make a quick getaway before the cops showed up. But he hadn't been the fastest guy around, certainly not in Swifte's league, and the police had eventually caught him and sent him to prison for his crimes. He'd done his time, gotten out a couple of years ago, and had been living on the streets ever since. These days, he went by Blue, and he wasn't a villain anymore, just a guy who'd fallen on hard times and was trying to get by.

I had first met Blue a couple of months ago when I'd been walking back to the office after lunch at Quicke's. I'd been carrying several bags of takeout food for Fiona, and Blue had been standing at the alley entrance, eyeing the sacks of burgers and fries, hunger shining bright in his eyes. So I'd given him all of Fiona's lunch that day, then gone back to the restaurant and bought him enough food for several more days as well.

After that, Blue had started hanging around the store, taking out the trash, packing up shipping boxes, and doing other chores for food and money. The two of us had slowly become friends, and I'd even interviewed him as part of my volunteer work with *A Bigtime Past*, the library's history project chronicling Bigtime's older heroes and villains and their impacts on the city. Blue had a lot of fascinating stories to tell, and I'd been happy to listen.

As we'd gotten to know each other, I'd tried to help him every way I could, even suggesting that he check out some of the city's homeless shelters. But Blue always refused, saying that he'd been taking care of himself all his life and saw no reason to stop now. So Fiona sewed clothes for him, making sure that he had plenty of warm gear for the winter, and I always made a pit stop in the alley on my way back from Quicke's and dropped off some food for him. Sometimes, I even ate lunch out here with Blue and listened to his stories about all the heroes and villains he'd had run-ins with over the years. Not just because I was recording them for the library but because his tales genuinely interested me. Kyle and Abby were both right. I was definitely a Fandemic with a capital F. Academic and epidemic and obsessive, all at once.

"Hey, Blue," I called out. "Hope we didn't disturb you. You know how rambunctious Rascal can be."

Instead of raising his head and greeting me, Blue remained still and quiet.

Unease twisted my stomach. "Blue? Are you okay?"

Rascal whined, sensing that something was wrong. I put

down my purse and the bag full of puppy supplies. Then I crept forward, bent down, and touched Blue's shoulder.

"Blue?" I asked again, shaking him a little bit. "Are you all right—"

Blue gasped and sucked down a giant gulp of air. He reached out and grabbed hold of my shoulder, his fingers digging painfully into my arm, despite my thick coat. Blue also had a bit of superstrength to go along with his speed.

"Get away from me, you monster!" he yelled. "Get away! Get away! Get away!"

"Blue!" I yelled back, trying to get him to listen to me. "It's Piper! Just Piper!"

He stared at me, his blue eyes dull and dark, but after a few seconds, he focused on me, and some of his panic and confusion faded away.

"Piper," he mumbled. "Piper...she'll know what to do...she'll know how to stop him...she knows everything about villains..."

"Blue?" I asked again. "Are you okay? What happened? Did someone hurt you?"

"Crept back here while I was sleeping...didn't think that I heard him...that I'd fight back..."

He mumbled a few more words, although I couldn't make out exactly what he was saying. His head lolled to the side, and it was my turn to gasp. All these horrible marks ringed Blue's neck, like someone had stuck a dozen needles into his throat and yanked them right back out again, leaving the skin there red, raw, and puckered. Some sort of thick, dark liquid was also oozing out from underneath his leg. I reached down, stuck my fingers into the liquid, and raised them back up to the dim light filtering in from the street.

Blood glistened on my hand.

"Blue!" I said, scooting even closer to him and trying to see where he might be hurt through all his many layers of clothes. "You're bleeding!"

He shuddered. "Blood, blood, all my blood. Down, down, down the drain, long gone…"

I pulled out my cell phone and started to call 911, but Blue seemed to realize what I was doing. He focused on me again, his fingers digging even deeper into my shoulder.

"He's a monster now," he muttered. "A monster! And he wants to kill us all. I heard him talking into his phone, taking notes about what he was doing to me. What he wants to do to everyone. Wings and snowflakes first…then swords and fire later…"

Blue leaned forward, clutching my coat with both hands. "You have to stop it. You have to stop *him*," he said, his voice getting louder and raspier with every word. "Or he'll rip it out of everyone. Wings and snowflakes…wings and snowflakes…"

He kept babbling that same phrase over and over again, although his voice got weaker and his hands slid free from my coat and dropped to his sides.

This time, I did call 911. I told the operator my situation, and she promised to send help immediately. I put my phone away, then focused on Blue again, patting him down and still trying to find the source of his bleeding.

Something had ripped through his coat and all the layers underneath it, right where his heart was. I peeled the fabric away as best I could, revealing several deep, jagged wounds that were dripping blood, as though Blue had been clawed by a bear or some other animal. A horrified gasp escaped from my lips.

So much blood.

Too much blood.

I ripped off my gloves and pressed them to the wounds, even though I knew how useless it was. And so did Blue.

"It's too late for that…" he rasped. "He clawed me too bad…"

I didn't have Abby's supersenses, but the coppery stink of his blood filled the alley, overpowering the garbage in all the trash cans. Rascal smelled it as well, and he kept pacing back and forth beside us, whining all the while.

"You're a good girl, Piper," Blue rasped. "You made this old man's life a lot easier these past few months."

"Don't talk like that that," I said, trying to inject some false cheer into my voice and failing miserably at it. "The paramedics are on their way. You're going to be fine. You'll be back here telling me more stories in no time flat. You'll see."

Blue smiled at me a final time, then his eyes went distant and glassy, his head lolled to the side again, and his entire body relaxed.

"Blue! Blue!" I yelled and yelled, but it was no use.

He died in my arms.

PART TWO

SUPERFAN

CHAPTER FIVE

The cops arrived about three minutes later. They found me in the back of the alley, cradling Blue's bloody body, with Rascal still whining and crying by my side. I was crying too, silent tears streaming down my face one after another.

I got to my feet and moved out of the way when the paramedics appeared, even though it was too late for Blue. Sure enough, a few minutes later, they pronounced him dead on the scene.

A cop walked me back out to the street, away from Blue's body, and took my statement. I told him everything I knew, and everything Blue had said to me before he'd died. Sometime during our conversation, I realized that Sean Newman, Bigtime's chief of police, had arrived and was listening to my story.

The officer finished taking my statement, retrieved my purse and bag of puppy supplies from the alley, and brought them over to me. I gave him my contact info in case he had any follow-up questions, then he went back into the alley with some of the other cops. I thought that Chief Newman would head back there as well, but instead he came over and put his hand on my shoulder.

"Are you okay, Piper?" he asked in his deep, Irish brogue.

I wiped another tear out of the corner of my eye. "It's just so sad, so horrible. Who would want to hurt Blue? He wasn't a villain. Not anymore. He was just a guy who was down on his luck."

At my feet, Rascal barked his agreement.

"I don't know who would do something like this," Chief Newman said. "But the entire department will work to find whoever murdered Bustling Blue and bring that person to justice."

I nodded. The chief always did his very best to keep his word, both in his day job and at night, when he was moonlighting as Mr. Sage. He was also Fiona's dad, a fact that few people knew, so I trusted him much more than he realized. Unlike earlier tonight with Wynter, I managed to keep my mouth shut and not blurt out his secret identity to everyone within earshot. Maybe my superfan brain was finally giving me a break.

Chief Newman stood by my side as Blue's body was placed on a stretcher and carted out of the alley. I wiped away a few more tears, while Rascal whined and whined, pressing his small, warm body against my legs and offering me what comfort he could.

The coroner had just loaded the body into the back of his van when the *screech-screech-screech* of tires sounded, and a SUV emblazoned with the Superhero News Network logo skidded to a stop at the corner, right where the ice cream truck had been parked before. The truck was gone now, and the cops had cordoned off the alley and the surrounding block with yellow crime scene tape.

The SUV had barely skidded to a stop before Kelly Caleb was out of the vehicle and striding toward the crime scene tape, a digital recorder clutched in her hands and her high heels *clack-clack-clacking* on the concrete sidewalk.

Chief Newman let out a loud, weary sigh. "Please excuse me, Piper," he rumbled. "I need to go prepare a statement for the press."

I nodded again, and he moved off to speak to one of the police department's public information officers who was on the scene. I wondered if Chief Newman was trying to put some sort of spin on Blue's death. If so, why? There might be dozens of heroes in Bigtime, but that didn't mean that the city was crime-free. Good Intentions Lane was proof enough of that. Even some of the villains wouldn't go into that neighborhood after dark. And muggings, robberies, murders, and more weren't just limited to the bad parts of the city. They could happen to anyone anywhere at any time.

Just like Blue's senseless death here tonight.

Kelly Caleb stopped at the yellow tape and looked at the chief, waving and trying to get his attention, but Newman turned his back, pointedly ignoring her. I frowned, wondering what she was doing here. Kelly was the star reporter for SNN, and I wouldn't think that the murder of a former, minor villain like Bustling Blue would blip this high on her radar, especially not this quickly.

Unless…there was something else going on here that I didn't know about.

Curious, I headed over to her.

Kelly saw me coming. She smiled and waved, and I waved back. Rascal followed along beside me. I ducked under the crime scene tape, and Kelly stepped forward and hugged me.

"Piper!" she said. "It's so good to see you!"

"You too, Kelly."

Kelly and I had gotten to know each other quite well when I'd been dating Kyle, since the two of them were cousins, along with Devlin "Debonair" Dash. Kelly was the only one of the three of them who didn't seem to have a superpower, though. At least, none that I'd ever seen her use, although I often wondered if she might really be Confidante, since Kelly got almost as many scoops as the comic book writer and artist did.

Kelly noticed my red, puffy eyes from when I'd been crying. She frowned. "What's wrong? Why are you here? Were you a witness to the murder?"

"Not to the murder, but I found Blue…afterward," I said, my throat closing up and tears welling in my eyes again. "It was…awful."

Kelly's face creased with sympathy. "I'm so sorry, Piper."

She squeezed my arm, but her sharp blue eyes had already taken on a speculative look.

"What are *you* doing here?" I asked. "And why does Chief Newman seem so determined to ignore you?"

The police chief was still standing with his back to us, although the information officer he was talking to kept glancing over at Kelly.

Kelly waved her hand, as though she were brushing off my concerns. "Oh, that's nothing new. I'm not the chief's favorite person. I never have been, and I never will be."

Her words were true enough, but the evasive tone in her voice told me that there was something else going on.

"What's wrong?" I asked. "Why are you really here? If you know something about what happened to Blue, please tell me. He was my friend, and I want whoever did this to be caught as soon as possible."

Kelly reached up and fluffed out her blond hair, buying herself some time to think about my request.

"Please," I said. "Tell me what you know."

Kelly quit messing with her hair. She hesitated a second longer, then crooked her finger at me. Curious, I followed her over to the SNN vehicle. Kelly glanced around to make sure that no one was listening or paying any attention to us. Then she opened the trunk, pulled a tablet out of a large black bag, and called up several photos on it.

"Someone's been going around the city killing heroes and villains," she said in a low voice.

She turned the screen around and swiped through several photos of various heroes and villains in their costumed glory days. I recognized all of them. Minor players in the supergame, all with

46

a variety of low-level powers. Radio Randall, a hero with enhanced senses. Muscular Mila, a hero with some extra strength. Catwalk, a former fashion-model-turned-villain who had the ability to summon up bright, blinding, camera-like flashes of light with her bare hands. She could also strut dramatically and yet still move without making a sound at the same time.

I knew these elderly heroes and villain especially well since I'd spent time with all of them recently, interviewing them for the library project. Nice folks, for the most part. Even Catwalk, although she'd been a little overly dramatic, wanting her story to be the focal point of the history project. They hadn't deserved to be murdered.

"And now, the not-so-nice photos," Kelly said. "Brace yourself. These aren't pretty."

I nodded, and she swiped through several more photos. Somehow, Kelly had gotten access to the crime-scene photos of the previous murders. Radio Randall, Muscular Mila, Catwalk. They all lay sprawled in their homes, eyes closed, as if they were asleep. But it was just a gruesome illusion. Nothing could hide the crimson blood spattered all over their clothes, the deep wounds crisscrossing their chests, and the ugly, red puncture marks in their necks—the same sort of wounds that had ringed Blue's throat.

My stomach twisted with horror and disgust, and more tears scalded my eyes, but I blinked them back and forced myself to focus on the images.

"What are those neck wounds?" I asked.

Kelly shrugged. "I don't know exactly, and neither does the coroner, according to my sources. But each victim was missing more than a pint of blood, according to the autopsy reports. The coroner suspects that it's some sort of collar made out of needles that was snapped around and then jabbed into their necks to help drain their blood as quickly as possible. Before they had a chance to fight back." She paused. "After their blood was taken, the killer finished them off by cutting them to pieces with some sort of knife."

Blue had fought back—he'd said as much—but the murderer had killed him anyway.

My hand crept up to my own neck, phantom pinpricks stinging my skin there. "How awful. But why would someone want to take a hero's or villain's blood…"

The answer was obvious.

"Their powers," I whispered. "Someone is going around Bigtime stealing superpowers."

Kelly nodded. "That's what it looks like. And that's what Chief Newman thinks too, even if I can't get him to say so on the record. But he let it slip to me that the Fearless Five are investigating the murders. They've been quietly warning other heroes and even the villains they encounter to watch their backs until they figure out who is doing this."

"But nobody warned Blue," I said in a sad voice. "And now it's too late."

Kelly winced. "I'm sorry, Piper. I remember you telling me how much you liked talking to him."

"I really did. Blue was always happy to share stories about all the heroes and other villains that he battled over the years. He said that it was a simpler time back then, that everything wasn't so carefully controlled and managed like it is today. That the heroes and villains could just be themselves and didn't have to worry about their brands or corporate images or fan bases." My throat closed up again, and my voice dropped to a whisper. "I'm going to miss him."

"Hey, Kelly!" A cameraman rounded the side of the SUV and jerked his thumb over his shoulder. "Newman's going to give a statement in another five minutes or so. Thought you might want to do a quick piece before he does, or before the folks from *The Chronicle* and *The Exposé* get here."

She nodded. "Thanks, Saul. I'll be right there."

Saul nodded back, grabbed some equipment out of the SUV, and lumbered off toward the crime scene tape.

48

"I'm sorry that I have to go," Kelly said. "Maybe we can grab lunch one day soon and catch up?"

"Sure. That would be great."

She smiled, then reached into the open trunk and pulled her black bag closer, unzipping the top and searching through the equipment inside. Something fell out of one of the side pockets and fluttered to the ground. Kelly didn't notice it, so I bent over and picked it up.

It was a single red rose, with a black ribbon tied to it. *See you soon* was printed in white letters on the ribbon, along with several small white hearts.

"Looks like someone has a secret admirer for Valentine's Day," I teased, holding the rose out to her.

Kelly looked up and gasped. Her blue eyes widened, and her pretty face paled as she stared and stared at the flower. She wet her lips, her gaze darting left and right, scanning the shadows around us as if she was afraid that someone was lurking in them, watching us.

Watching *her.*

"Where did you get that?" she asked, her voice a low, ragged whisper.

"It was in your bag," I said. "It fell out of one of the side pockets."

Kelly snatched the rose out of my hand and stared at the message printed on the black ribbon. For a moment, her hand trembled, but then her mouth hardened into a flat line. She marched over to the trash can at the corner and tossed the flower inside before spinning around and storming back over to me.

"I take it that's not from a Valentine," I said.

"Not even close." Kelly shook her head. "It's nothing. Just a...present from an...overeager fan."

"It doesn't look like nothing to me," I said in a gentle voice. "Do you want to talk about it?"

She gave me a wide smile, but her eyes were dark and troubled.

"Don't worry. I can handle it. This isn't the first time someone's left me a…present like this, and I doubt it will be the last."

Kelly grabbed a wireless microphone and some more equipment from her bag, closed the SUV trunk, and went over to her cameraman, who had already set up in front of the yellow crime scene tape. Saul adjusted his camera lens and turned on the light on top of the device, while Kelly checked that her microphone was working properly. When everything was ready, Kelly positioned herself in front of the crime scene tape, with the red and blue lights of the police cars flashing on the street behind her.

"In three," Saul said, pointing at her. "Three, two, one…"

Kelly tightened her grip on her microphone and stared straight into the camera, her face serious. "Good evening. This is Kelly Caleb with the Superhero News Network reporting from the scene of yet another grisly murder on the streets of Bigtime. We'll be hearing from Chief Sean Newman in a few minutes with some more details of the brutal crime, but here's what we know so far…"

Kelly went into full-fledged reporter mode, recapping all the facts.

I watched her for several minutes, but everything she said just made me feel that much more melancholy and heartbroken. Blue hadn't deserved to be killed for his speed power. And neither had any of the other victims.

At my feet, Rascal let out a small, sad bark.

"Yeah, boy. That's just how I feel too." I sighed. "Let's go home."

We reached my apartment about fifteen minutes later. I unlocked the door and let myself in. I removed Rascal's collar and leash, and the puppy bounded forward, sniffing everything in sight. I put down my things, stripped off my bloody, ruined coat, and stood in the kitchen, staring out over the rest of my apartment.

Superhero memorabilia stretched out from wall to wall and from the front to the back of my apartment. A wide range of heroes were represented on everything from the Swifte clock hanging on the kitchen wall to the thought-a-day Mr. Sage calendar sitting on the coffee table to the Fiera electric blanket that was crumpled up at one end of my couch. Practically everything I owned had some sort of hero, symbol, or official logo on it. There were even a few villain-themed items in the mix, like the Caveman Stan zebra-stripe kitchen towels that Abby had bought me as a gag gift for Christmas.

Normally, I loved coming home to my apartment, to all the cool and quirky things I'd collected over the years. But tonight, the sight of all the memorabilia just depressed me.

Especially the vintage Bustling Blue lunch box sitting on the kitchen counter.

I walked over, reached out, and traced my fingers over Blue's smiling masked face. I had found the metal box last week at the downtown comic book store. I had been planning to shine it up, pop the dents out of it, and give it to Blue, since I knew that he'd get a kick out of it.

But it was too late now.

Another wave of sadness rippled through me, and I dropped my hand from the box.

I still had Rascal to take care of, so I put out some food and water for him, as well as arranging his wicker basket in the corner and scattering his chew toys all around it. The puppy slurped down some water, had a mouthful of kibble, and curled up in his bed. He must have been as exhausted as I was because a minute later, he was asleep, his brown, furry paws twitching as he dreamed about bounding after something.

It was late, and I needed to go to bed too, so I grabbed my

coat, which was covered with Blue's blood, and balled it up so I could stuff it into my Hermit trash can. Something slid out of one of the coat pockets and fluttered to the floor. I picked it up and realized that it was the bit of jagged, torn fabric I'd found in the alley. Just like I'd suspected, it was a shimmering ice-blue, although the edges of the fabric were stained with what looked like blood.

I frowned. Fiona absolutely loathed ice-blue, and none of the clothes she had made for Blue had been even close to this color. So where—or *who*—might the scrap of fabric have come from?

Had…had Blue's murderer dropped it?

Blue had said that he'd fought back against his killer. Maybe he'd put up more of a struggle than I'd realized. Maybe he'd even managed to rip the other person's clothes.

The gears in my brain started grinding together, and I turned on my laptop on the kitchen table, which was embossed with the Fearless Five logo. I washed my hands and microwaved myself some dark hot chocolate while I waited for the laptop to boot up. Once they were both ready, I sat down at the table, scrolled through my files, and clicked on one titled *Fandemic*.

Documents, photos, voice recordings, and more popped up onto my screen, all part of *A Bigtime Past*, the library's project chronicling Bigtime's heroes and villains. I had been planning to volunteer to help with the project anyway, but after Kyle had dumped me, I'd thrown myself wholeheartedly into it. Working on the project hadn't helped me get over Kyle and our breakup, but it had kept me from sitting in my apartment and moping for hours on end. And it had been more fun than I'd thought possible.

I had always loved facts and figures and learning obscure bits of information, so something like the history project was right up my alley. I'd become so interested in Bigtime's superhistory that I had done some extra research, just for my own enjoyment, digging up old photos of heroes and villains from the *Chronicle* and *Exposé* newspapers, reading about hero-and-villain rivalries in the library archives, and even doing a spreadsheet of all the city buildings that had been destroyed in various battles and how much it had cost to repair them. (Five hundred billion and counting, by my estimates.)

But my favorite part of the project had been tracking down former heroes and villains, interviewing them, and recording all their wild, fascinating stories about past battles, feuds, and more. Most of them were retired from crime-fighting or committing and had been happy to talk about their time roaming the streets of Bigtime. For some of them, it had brought up fond memories they hadn't thought about in years.

Clicking through the photos made me think about that phrase Blue had kept repeating before he'd died. *Wings and snowflakes... Wings and snowflakes...*

I frowned. Could his words have been a warning? Practically every hero and villain identified themselves with some sort of symbol or logo. I wondered if Blue had been talking about other people's symbols, other folks who might be the killer's next targets.

So I went online, logged on to the web page and database for the library's history project, and typed the words *wings* and *snowflakes* into the search engine. More than three dozen hits popped up on my screen. Heroes and villains loved symbols, and wings and snowflakes were some of the more popular ones, since so many superfolks could fly or had cold-based powers.

I scrolled through page after page of information. Talon, Johnny Angel, Snow Globe, the Winged Whistler... The list went on and on, although two very familiar names kept popping up over and over again.

Swifte and Wynter.

I frowned again. Swifte's speed and Wynter's strength and icy abilities. Those would be good powers to have. No, scratch that. They would be *great* ones to have. So would the powers of all the other heroes and villains on the list. The killer could be targeting anyone in the database, anyone in Bigtime, but I kept clicking back to the information on Swifte and Wynter.

Maybe I was way off target, but I couldn't help the uneasy feeling that slithered up my spine at the thought that Kyle and Sabrina might be in danger. Sabrina was my friend, and Kyle, well, I didn't know what Kyle and I were right now, but I still cared about him. I couldn't just sit around and do nothing. I'd have to warn them both tomorrow. Even if Chief Newman and the rest of the Fearless Five had put the word out about the murders to all the heroes in town, I wanted Kyle and Sabrina to hear it again from me. It was the only way that I would feel better about things.

Since I couldn't figure out who the killer might be targeting next, I turned my attention to my only other clue—that bloody scrap of ice-blue fabric. At least, that's what color I thought it was, although I couldn't find an exact match in any of my information or the library's database. Blue was a popular color among heroes and villains, varying from the bright cobalt that Talon wore to Wynter's pale costume.

I was no detective, but Blue had said that I would know what to do. That I would know how to stop his killer. I hadn't been able to save my friend, but maybe—just maybe—I could help bring his murderer to justice. I didn't want Blue's faith in me to be wasted. Otherwise, I would have failed him all over again.

So I stared and stared at the fabric. If I could just figure out whose costume it had come from, maybe I would know who was targeting the other heroes and villains and keep anyone else from getting hurt.

My eyes narrowed, and a smile curved my face. I didn't need the library's database to find the exact color of the fabric because I had access to something even better and far more precise— Fiona Fine.

Nobody knew their fabric colors and swatches like she did.

And since she moonlighted as Fiera, she was familiar with all the city's heroes and villains, including their costumes. Over the years, I had heard both Fiona and Fiera critiquing other heroes' and villains' outfits. In her book, Kyle, Swifte, was one of the worst offenders. Fiona had a very, very strong belief that no one should wear shiny, opalescent white from head to toe. As much as I loved Kyle and Swifte, I didn't think she was completely wrong about that.

So if this scrap of fabric had indeed come from someone's costume, then Fiona would know exactly whose, and she could pass the information on to Chief Newman and the rest of the Fearless Five. Then the police and the heroes could start homing in on Blue's killer.

Satisfied with my plan, I shut down my laptop to finally take a shower and go to bed.

CHAPTER SIX

My phone chiming with a text from Abby woke me up the next morning.

Help! Wesley keeps taking away my phone. He doesn't understand how important it is for me to check my messages—

The text cut off, as though Wesley had plucked the phone out of Abby's hand. I stared at my own phone, betting that I'd get another message. Sure enough, it chimed again a second later.

Abby wants to know how Rascal is. She is *not* turning her phone back on again today. W.

I smiled and texted them back. *Rascal is fine. Enjoy your vacation! XOXO. P.*

I waited again, but I didn't get another text. Maybe Wesley really would get Abby to turn off her phone, at least for a few hours. I smiled again and got out of bed.

Rascal bounded out of his basket and chowed down on some puppy kibble, while I slipped his collar and leash on him, put on several layers of thick, warm clothes myself, and got ready for work. The fabric scrap was tucked away in my purse, and I bagged up some supplies for Rascal, including his favorite Swifte chew toy, since the puppy was coming to work with me.

My first stop was Bryn's Bakery, where I bought four dozen assorted doughnuts, along with four dozen bagels, half blueberry and half cinnamon-raisin, and enough cream cheese to slather from here to Ashland. Fiona was always extra-hungry in the mornings, and I figured that it wouldn't hurt to have several bags of food in hand to bribe her into identifying the mystery fabric for me.

It was ten o'clock by the time I made it to Fiona Fine Fashions, and the clerks had just opened up the storefront when I strolled inside, with Rascal trotting along beside me, eagerly sniffing the floor. Fiona didn't believe in opening too early, since she almost always needed a couple more hours of sleep in the morning, given all her late nights moonlighting as Fiera.

The storefront's floor and walls were white and completely bare of decoration, all the better to show off the racks of designer dresses, shelves full of shoes, and counters crammed full of jewelry, purses, and other accessories. Fiona didn't believe in being subtle either, and all her designs from the dresses to the shoes to the bags were big, bold, and brightly colored. With polka dots, neon feathers, and flashing jewels to boot. Sometimes, all the bright colors, loud patterns, and glittering gemstones gave me a headache, but people loved Fiona's daring designs, which kept me employed, so I couldn't complain too much.

Rock music pulsed in the background, and a couple of models had already started strutting their stuff on the runway in the center of the store. This week, Fiona had decided to show off designs from her summer rock-glam collection, which meant lots of black and pink leather, lots of silver chains, and lots of musical accents, like silver guitars and white velvet music notes.

I stopped to talk to Jess, the clerk running the store today. She let out a squeal of delight and came around the checkout counter to pet Rascal before straightening up and eyeing the bulging bags of food I had slung over my shoulder.

"Did Fiona send you out for food already?" she asked.

"Fiona's here?"

She nodded. "And not in a good mood. She's been growling at everyone. But maybe the food will help. It always seems to."

Jess kept staring at the bags of food. A couple of years ago, she'd jokingly remarked that Fiona must be a superhero to eat as much as she did and never gain a pound. Everyone in the storefront had heard her, clerks and customers alike, and I could almost see the wheels turning in their minds as they thought about Fiona being a superhero and who she might be masquerading as. Just the way that Jess was thinking about it again right now.

I didn't want to blow my boss's secret identity, and I'd been so desperate to get everyone talking about something else that I'd blurted out the first thing that came to mind—that Fiona had an eating disorder.

I felt terrible about it, since eating disorders were nothing to make light of. But to my surprise, my spur-of-the-moment lie had actually worked. Everyone's faces had immediately softened with sympathy, and they had all started nodding their heads and murmuring to themselves. *Of course she does. That explains so much. The poor thing. I hope that Fiona gets the help she needs...*

So I had kept up the charade, even going so far as to make sure that all the clerks and workers knew that I put pamphlets about eating disorders and treatment clinics on Fiona's desk from time to time. Fiona thought I was crazy, but she didn't realize how close she came to blowing her secret identity every time she ordered a massive amount of food from Quicke's or some other nearby restaurant. Which she did on a daily basis.

"Is she really going to eat all those doughnuts?" Jess whispered.

"Well, you know Fiona. She has a...strange relationship with food."

Jess shook her head. "It's so sad."

"Don't worry," I said, lying through my teeth. "I've been talking to her about it, and I think Fiona is finally ready to admit that she has a problem."

Jess's face brightened. "That's good."

"Yeah. Good."

I went over to the door set in the wall, punched in my code, and stepped into the back, with Rascal still trotting along by my side. This was the factory portion of the building, where all of Fiona's flamboyant designs were produced. Workers sat at tables, sewing everything from evening gowns to sweaters to doggie tuxedoes, since Fiona was getting ready to launch her new petwear evening line this fall. I waved at everyone and put two boxes each of the doughnuts and bagels out for the workers to share. Then I took the remaining food to my office.

A desk, a laptop, some printers, several chairs, filing cabinets lining the walls. My office was your typical corporate space, except for my Karma Girl fountain pen and the Swifte note pads that were stuck to my monitor, reminding me about various deadlines and other things I needed to check on. But for the most part, I left the superheroes at home. Here, I was all business.

I put out some food and water for Rascal, along with a large pillow for him to sleep on and his Swifte chew toy. While the puppy was busy sniffing every corner of my office, I fired up my laptop and checked my e-mail, taking care of a few pressing matters right off the bat. When I was caught up on everything that needed my immediate attention, I surfed over to the SNN website and pulled up all of Kelly Caleb's reports about the recent hero-villain murders. But there was nothing on the site that Kelly hadn't already told me, so I plucked the fabric scrap out of my purse, gathered up the boxes of doughnuts and bagels, and headed next door to Fiona's office.

Fiona Fine was sitting in her chair, a sketch pad in hand and colored pencils scattered all over the top of her desk. Rolls of fabric covered the chairs in front of her desk, while mannequins draped with necklaces, hats, and billowing swaths of silk were stuffed into the corners of the room.

Fiona sat in the middle of the mess, her feet up on the desk, clutching a neon-pink pencil in her hand and *tap-tap-tapping* it against the sketch pad, as if waiting for inspiration to strike. She was gorgeous, with long blond hair, blue eyes, and a figure that was perfect for modeling all the outrageous designs she created. Fiona wore an electric-blue turtleneck sweater with black-and-white zebra-stripe leggings and black stiletto ankle boots, but the odd mix of colors and patterns looked as fabulous on her as everything else did.

She looked up at the sound of my footsteps, along with Rascal's toenails *click-click-clicking* on the floor. The puppy went over and plopped down beside the desk, staring up at Fiona with wide eyes. Despite all the times he'd been in her office, Rascal always seemed surprised by how colorful she was. He wasn't the only one.

"Good morning," I chirped.

"Hmph."

Fiona glowered at me, and an errant, red-hot spark shot out of her thumb, one that I pretended not to see, even though it landed on a stack of papers shoved off to one side of her desk and started to smolder. Fiona was *so* not a morning person.

So I put the boxes of doughnuts and bagels on top of her already messy desk. That made her perk right up. Without a word, Fiona opened one of the boxes, stuffed a chocolate-covered doughnut in her mouth, and practically swallowed it whole. I pulled my phone out of my pocket and checked my messages, waiting until she downed half a dozen doughnuts and several bagels before I shoved the fabric rolls off a chair in front of her desk and sat down in it.

"Good morning," I repeated.

"Mmm-hmm," Fiona echoed my greeting through a mouthful of blueberry bagel.

"I was wondering if you could take a look at something for me."

Fiona raised her eyebrows, a powdered doughnut clutched in either hand. On the floor, Rascal whined, hoping that she would drop one of the sweet treats so he could gobble it up. Heh. Fat chance of that happening. Fiona never let food escape her grasp that easily.

"I did bring you doughnuts after all," I said, my voice taking on a wheedling note. "With bagels and cream cheese. I think that officially makes me the best CFO ever. Not to mention a really good friend too."

Fiona dusted the powdered sugar off her hands. "Well, I suppose that I could do you this one small favor." She looked at the clock on the wall, and her stomach growled, despite all the food she'd just eaten. "When are you going to Quicke's for lunch?"

"Soon," I promised. "Now, about that favor…"

Fiona sighed, grabbed the final jelly-filled doughnut out of the box, and leaned back in her chair. "Hit me."

I placed the fabric scrap on her desk. She crammed the doughnut into her mouth, then snatched up the fabric, holding it up to the light.

"Can you tell me what color that is?" I asked, hope rising in my chest.

Fiona scoffed. "That's easy. Ice-blue forty-two."

I blinked. "Ice-blue forty-two? As in, there are forty-one *other* colors of ice-blue?"

"Actually, there are fifty-seven distinctive colors of ice-blue," Fiona said. "At least, those are the ones officially recognized by the Bigtime Fashion Designers Association. But then you have your rogue designers who are always coming up with their own crazy color combinations…"

And she was off and running, all that sugar in her system making her face light up as she started describing each and every one of the subtle differences between all fifty-seven shades of ice-blue. My eyes glazed over, and it was only a whine from Rascal that finally roused me enough to interrupt her.

"Do you know anyone who uses that particular color of ice-blue?" I asked, trying to figure out how to subtly ask her which villain might wear a costume that was that color.

Fiona wrinkled her nose. "Ice-blue? I would never, *ever* use ice-blue. It's not nearly colorful enough, not nearly bold enough. You should make a statement with your clothes. Not dress up like a washed-out icicle."

She gestured at her turtleneck sweater. "Now this? *This* is a color. It's electric-blue twenty-two. Isn't it fabulous?"

Fiona tossed her long blond hair over her shoulder so I could get a better look at her sweater, as if it weren't searing my eyes with its intense hue.

"Yeah, fabulous," I echoed in a faint voice.

"But even if I were suddenly going to lose my mind and design a collection that featured a pale color palette, I would never, *ever* use ice-blue forty-two." Fiona sniffed.

"Why not? What's wrong with it?"

She shrugged. "Because Frost always used that color for his costume."

Frost.

My blood chilled at the ubervillain's name. Frost was one of the worst of the worst, the kind of monster that even the other villains were afraid of. Frost fancied himself a scientist, and he was always conducting some sort of gruesome experiments on animals. People too, from the rumors I'd heard. If anyone was going around Bigtime murdering people and stealing their powers, Frost would be the perfect candidate. Not only did he have the scientific know-how to do it, but he was absolutely evil that way too.

I wet my lips. "But Frost is dead, right? Weren't he and the other members of the Terrible Triad killed in that big explosion at the Snowdom Ice Cream Factory a while back?"

Fiona shrugged again. "That's what the Fearless Five reported. But you know ubervillains. They're harder to kill than cockroaches. They always seem to come back from the dead every few years."

She looked at the swatch again. "But what's this stain on the fabric? Is that...dried blood?"

"I think so," I said. "I found the swatch in the alley beside the store when I was walking home last night. Along with Blue."

Fiona frowned. "Blue? Has something happened to Blue?"

I didn't know if she was playing dumb or if she just hadn't heard the news yet. "He's dead."

I drew in a breath and told her about finding Blue last night. Fiona's eyes narrowed, and several more red-hot sparks shot out of her thumbs before she curled her hands into fists to hide the errant sparks from me. I told her everything I knew, including the strange warnings that Blue had mentioned about wings and snowflakes and how I suspected that he might be talking about Swifte and Wynter being the killer's next targets.

When I finished, Fiona picked up her pencil and started *tap-tap-tapping* it on her sketch pad again.

"If Frost is back and stealing powers from other heroes and villains..."

Her voice trailed off, but she didn't have to finish her thought. We both knew how bad that would be. Frost was dangerous enough on his own. If he was collecting powers, he could quickly become unstoppable.

I cleared my throat, and Fiona focused on me again.

"Anyway, I was thinking that maybe you could call Chief Newman and tell him about all of this. I told him most of it last night, but I forgot about finding the fabric scrap. And of course I didn't know about Frost using that color for his costume until you told me just now. But it wouldn't hurt for the chief to hear it all again, especially from you."

She frowned again, and a suspicious light flared in her blue eyes. "And why would you think that *I* should tell Chief Newman about this?"

Because he's your father and superhero teammate!

That's what I wanted to scream, since it was so freaking *obvious* and I had known it for *so long now*. But instead, I plastered a bland smile on my face the way I always did whenever I was playing dumb. "Oh, you know, because you're such a prominent citizen. He'll listen to you. And all the heroes and villains should be warned if Frost is back in Bigtime. Don't you think?"

Fiona's frown deepened, but she didn't argue with my logic. Instead, she grabbed the last blueberry bagel out of the box and shoved it into her mouth.

"I guess you're right," she said, after chewing and swallowing the entire bagel in five seconds flat. "I'll give him a call right now."

I smiled again. "Great. I really appreciate it."

Fiona waved her hand. "No problem."

I grabbed the fabric swatch off her desk, took hold of Rascal's leash, and went back to my office. I had just unhooked the puppy's leash from his collar and sat down at my desk when I heard Fiona punch in some numbers on her phone. A minute later, she started talking in a not-so-quiet voice.

"Hey, Chief, it's me. Listen, Piper was just in my office. She found something interesting at your crime scene last night…"

Fiona told him everything I'd asked her to. Our offices were off by themselves in the very back of the building, so I was the only one who could hear her. I shook my head. That was how I'd found out that Fiona was really Fiera in the first place. She was always calling one member of the Fearless Five about something or other, or asking Lulu Lo to come over and help with our computers.

I fired up my laptop again and tried to do some work. There were a hundred things I needed to accomplish today, just like there were every day at *FFF*. But instead, I found myself staring at that scrap of fabric again. I don't know why, but the longer I looked at the fabric, the more worried I got about Swifte. He was the fastest hero in all of Bigtime, and if Frost somehow got his power...

But even more than that, I was worried about Kyle. I loved him, and I didn't want him to get hurt. The Fearless Five might be putting the word out about Frost stealing superpowers, but I wanted to warn Kyle too.

My hand hovered over my phone. It would be easy for me to pick up the phone and call him. I'd long ago memorized the number to Quicke's, since I dialed it at least once a day to get food delivered for Fiona.

But seeing Kyle last night...him saving me from that falling spotlight...talking to him on the street...and then watching Blue die...knowing that I couldn't save my friend...

It had all reminded me that life was short—too short not to be with the people you cared about—and it had renewed my determination to win him back. It was silly, the reason we'd broken up, and we'd already been apart for far too long. It was time to convince Kyle that I loved him for *him*, and not because he was a superhero. It was time for us to get back together—for good.

So I leaned to the side of my desk and looked down at Rascal. "Hey, boy. You want to go for a walk?"

The puppy barked and bounded up off his pillow. I grinned. That was definitely a *yes*.

I clipped Rascal's leash to his collar again, stuck my head in Fiona's office, and told her that I was heading over to Quicke's for an early lunch. She waved her hand, distracted by the doodles on her sketch pad. I wondered if she might include some ice-blue in her next collection after all. No doubt she would combine it with some weird combinations that totally worked, like pink feathers, silver sequins, and black crystals.

I grabbed my purse, coat, and gloves and headed outside. I didn't think it was possible, but the temperature had dropped during the short time I'd been in the office, and it was even colder outside than before. The weather made me think of Frost, which sent another chill racing down my spine.

I fell into the flow of foot traffic on the sidewalks and hurried over to Quicke's. The sight of the neon-blue sign flashing above the revolving door always brought a smile to my face. I pushed through the door, stopped inside the entrance, and breathed in. I might not have Abby's supersense of smell, but the delicious aromas of fried chicken, macaroni and cheese, and fresh bread permeated the entire restaurant. My stomach growled. Fiona wasn't the only one who could use some food. I'd skipped breakfast to swing by Bryn's Bakery, and I hadn't had the chance to swipe a doughnut or bagel for myself before Fiona had inhaled them all.

Ray, the head waiter, was working the seating station, and he led me over to the best table in the restaurant, one that fronted the windows. I told him to go ahead and deliver my usual order to Fiona's office. If things went the way I wanted them to with Kyle, then I wouldn't be going back to work today. Ray moved off to take my order to the kitchen, and I leaned back in my seat and stared out over the restaurant.

Quicke's was known for its great food, hearty portions, and affordable prices, but it was most famous for being a shrine to all things superhero and ubervillain. The Fearless Five, the Terrible Triad, Johnny Angel, Debonair, the Mintilator, Siren, and Intelligal. Framed posters, photos, and newspaper clippings of heroes and villains covered the restaurant's brick walls, while toys, miniature cars, action figures, and more decorated the mirrored shelves running behind the long, brass-railed bar.

Even though I came in here several times a week, I never got tired of looking at all the photos and memorabilia. Kyle and I used to spend hours browsing through antique and other shops all over Bigtime, looking for even more knickknacks to add to the restaurant. Those trips and all the fun we'd had on them were yet another thing that I missed about him.

A poster of Talon loomed on the wall above my head, causing Rascal to bark and wag his tail.

"Sorry, boy," I said. "Talon will be back in a few days."

Rascal whined his disappointment and put his head down onto his paws. But I rubbed his ears, which made him raise his head right back up in happiness. Even though petting him made my allergies kick into high gear, I sneezed and kept right on rubbing the puppy's ears.

In addition to the photos and memorabilia, the other thing that Quicke's had going for it was the fact that it was considered neutral territory, one of the few places in the city where heroes and villains could hang out without fear of reprisals from one another or even the police. Even though it was still a little early for lunch, more than one spandex-clad person was already inside the restaurant. Halitosis Hal and Pistol Pete, the heroes who were best friends, were chowing down on some spaghetti and meatballs at a nearby table, while Gentleman George was perched on a barstool, dabbing at some stain he'd gotten on his peach ascot. A couple of other seats at the bar were empty, although two glasses clinked together in mid-air before slowly tipping back and the liquid inside them disappearing. The Invisible Ingénues were staked out there.

And Wynter was here too, sitting at the far end of the bar, sipping a fizzy blue soda and noshing on a plate of mozzarella sticks. Rascal was snoozing on the floor, so I got up from my chair and walked over to her.

"We meet again," I said.

Wynter looked at me. "Hey, Pip— Oh, er, *you*."

Once again, she was pretending like she didn't know who I was, but I decided to roll with it.

"I need to talk to you about something."

"What?"

I drew in a breath and told her everything that had happened with Blue last night, including his warning about wings and snowflakes, and what Fiona had told me about the fabric scrap probably belonging to Frost.

When I finished, Wynter frowned at me the same way Fiona had earlier. "So you think that Frost is back in town and stealing powers from other heroes and villains before he kills them? And that I'm next on his hit list?"

I shrugged. "I know there are a lot of folks who use snowflakes as symbols, but you're one of the strongest."

She patted her blond hair, preening a little at my compliment.

"Anyway, I wanted to come over and warn you," I said. "Just in case you were out at Oodles o' Stuff, working late tonight."

Wynter gave me a suspicious look. "Oodles o' Stuff, huh?"

Instead of saying that it was where Sabrina St. John, her real self, worked, I just shrugged again.

She polished off her last mozzarella stick and the rest of her soda. "Thanks, Pip— Oh, er, *you*. I'll take it under advisement."

Wynter gave me one more suspicious look, then paid her bill and left the restaurant.

I stepped into the bathroom, washed my hands, and made it back over to my table just in time for Ray to set my food down in front of me. Given the cold, dreary day, I'd wanted some warm, hearty comfort food, and Quicke's always delivered on that. I leaned over my plate, breathing in the succulent smells rising up from the chili I'd ordered, along with cornbread and a large baked potato stuffed with sharp cheddar cheese, sour cream, crispy bacon, and sliced green onions.

I dug into my food, which tasted even better than it smelled.

The chili was a terrific mix of spicy meat, hearty beans, and rich broth, while the cornbread was crusty on the outside and light and fluffy on the inside. And the melting cheese and other fixings were the perfect toppers for the baked potato.

I washed it all down with a glass of sweet iced tea while I scanned the restaurant, looking for Kyle. But he wasn't working the seating station like usual, and I didn't spot him at the bar or moving through the restaurant, taking orders and waiting on tables. I finished my food, and when Ray came back with my check, I asked him where Kyle was.

Ray jerked his thumb over his shoulder. "He's been in the kitchen, cooking, all morning long."

I frowned. Kyle enjoyed cooking, but what he loved most was being out front, right in the middle of the action, and interacting with all the folks who came to Quicke's in search of a good meal. He only stayed in the kitchen and threw himself into cooking if he was upset about something. And I was willing to bet that something was me, given how we'd left things last night.

Ray had long ago memorized the numbers on my Fiona Fine Fashions corporate credit card, so I signed the slip he gave me and added a generous tip for him. Then I grabbed Rascal's leash, crossed the storefront, pushed through the swinging double doors, and stepped into the back of the restaurant.

In many ways, Quicke's kitchen was just like the front of the restaurant, in that hero and villain posters and photos were plastered all over the walls. Stickers shaped like various hero and villain logos covered many of the stainless-steel appliances, and still more logos and symbols could be found on everything from the dish towels to the staff's aprons to the chefs' hats.

Kyle was standing in front of a series of stoves set in the middle of the kitchen, cooking, stirring, and flipping food from one hot pan and plate to another. There were plenty of other folks back here, including three other cooks and several waiters, but Kyle was the one doing the majority of the work, moving from one station to the other and back again almost too fast to follow. Everyone else was focused on what they were doing, or they would have noticed their boss's quick movements. Or maybe they were just so used to seeing him move so fast that it simply didn't register with them anymore how swift he actually was.

For a moment, I stood by the double doors and just watched him, admiring his smooth, efficient movements as he grilled a burger, then heaped lasagna onto a plate, then topped off a chocolate pie with whipped cream and dark chocolate sauce. Memories of him doing all those things and more flashed through my mind, and my lips curved into a soft smile. I had spent many a late night back here, sipping a glass of wine while Kyle cooked us both dinner and we told each other about our days. That companionship, that closeness, was something else that I missed about him, and something else that I was determined to get back.

Kyle must have sensed my gaze because he looked up and froze, a metal pan dangling from his hand at a sharp angle and the chocolate pie inside threatening to slide right out of the dish and plop onto the floor. But Kyle realized that he was in danger of losing the pie. From one blink to the next, he straightened the pan in his hand, drizzled a bit more chocolate sauce over the pie, and handed the whole thing off to one of his waiters.

Kyle wiped his hands on a towel, then left the stoves behind and came over to me.

"Piper?" he asked. "What are you doing here? Is something wrong?"

Even though we'd been apart these past few months, he still knew me better than almost anyone else.

"We need to talk." I lowered my voice. "About your *other* job."

Kyle grimaced at my not-so-subtle words, but whatever he saw in my face must have convinced him that it was important.

"Okay," he said. "I have an appointment that I need to get to anyway. Let's take a walk. Guys, I'll be back in a couple of hours."

The cooks and waiters all nodded at him. Kyle nodded back, then walked through the kitchen, grabbed a black duffel bag out of a locker along the wall, and went out the back of the restaurant.

I tightened my grip on Rascal's leash and followed him, wondering if this would be the most important conversation of our entire relationship.

CHAPTER SEVEN

Kyle stepped out into the alley. I followed him, with Rascal trotting along beside me, and he shut the door behind us.

The cold blasted over my face, feeling especially brutal after the intense heat of the kitchen. I shivered and turned up the collar of my coat, but Kyle stuck his hands in his pants pockets, despite the fact that he was only wearing sneakers, jeans, and a T-shirt patterned with Swifte's wings logo that I'd given him for his birthday, back before we'd broken up. The weather never seemed to bother him. Sometimes, I thought that he could simply outrun the cold if he really wanted to.

Kyle and I stood there for a minute, not quite looking at each other. Finally, he raised his gaze to mine and jerked his thumb over his shoulder.

"I really do have an appointment to get to at Paradise Park," he said, giving me a crooked smile. "Abby booked me for one of her hero meet-and-greet events. She'll kill me if I don't show up on time. So if you don't mind…"

He gestured at the duffel bag hanging off his shoulder.

"Go ahead," I said. "Your secret's safe with me."

Kyle nodded. He looked up and down the alley to make sure we were alone. Then—

WHOOSH!

A gust of wind blasted over me, tangling my hair and fluffing out Rascal's fur, making the puppy bark in surprise.

One second, Kyle Quicke was standing in front of me in jeans and a T-shirt. I blinked, and Swifte was there, shimmering in his white costume. My gaze traced over his body. Kyle was tall and lean, but he had plenty of muscles in *all* the right places, and he filled out that spandex very, very well.

Heat rippled through my body as I remembered his kiss, his touch, and all the ways he'd made me melt in the dark when we were together. Something else I'd missed about him. Kyle might be the fastest man in Bigtime, but there were certain instances where he *always* took his time—

"Piper?" Kyle asked. "Are you getting sick? Your cheeks are really red all of a sudden."

My hands darted up to my face. "It must be the cold." I cleared my throat. "Can I walk you over to the park? We can talk on the way. If that's okay with you?"

He nodded, hid his duffel bag behind one of the trash cans, and headed out to the main street. I fell in step beside him, with Rascal trotting along at my heels. The three of us slowly ambled over to Paradise Park, which was only a few blocks from the restaurant. Many folks eyed Kyle, since he was wearing his superhero suit, but no one stopped to take his picture or ask him for an autograph. They didn't think he was really Swifte, since he wasn't racing around town.

I opened and closed my mouth half a dozen times, trying to figure out where to begin. But every time I gathered up my courage to start talking, I mashed my lips together again.

Come on, Piper! I chided myself. Kyle could zoom away at any second, and I needed to tell him what was going on. I owed it to him, and especially to Blue. So I opened my mouth and forced out the words.

"Have you always had your powers? Why did you become a superhero? What do you love about it?"

The questions tumbled from my lips one after another. I winced. That wasn't what I had intended to say—not at *all*—but those were some of the many questions that had been running through my mind ever since I'd found out that Kyle was also Swifte. Maybe it was my inner superfan, but I wanted to know absolutely everything about Kyle *and* Swifte.

Startled, Kyle looked at me, not sure what to make of the sudden deluge.

My cheeks burned again, but there was no taking it back, so I forced myself to keep on talking. "Sorry, I didn't mean for all that to come out quite that way. I just want to know why you do...the things you do. Please."

A ghost of a smile flitted across his face. "I suppose you deserve that, after everything that's happened."

We stopped at the corner and waited for the walk sign to light up. Kyle drew in a deep breath, as if he enjoyed the scent of car exhaust mixed with the jumbo pretzels that the food truck at the curb was selling. Rascal was only interested in the pretzels, his small black nose quivering as he stared at the display case full of the salty treats.

The light changed to walk, but Kyle stood still, as if he were drinking in the ebb and flow of all the people moving around us, along with the *honk-honk* of car horns and *jangle-jangle* of bicycles zipping down the sidewalks.

"*This*," he finally said, holding his hands out wide. "This city, these people, all the sights and sounds and smells and pure *energy*. It's like a bigger version of the restaurant, and I love it. I love being right in the middle of things. I love helping people, talking to them..."

"And posing for photos?" I added in a dry tone.

Kyle laughed, his face lighter and happier than I'd seen in a long time. "*Especially* posing for photos. I was always the class clown in school, the guy who loved being the center of attention. Being a superhero seemed like a natural outlet for all that energy."

"Well, that certainly explains all the opalescent white," I said, falling into the old familiar rhythm of teasing him. "There's no missing you in that costume."

He laughed again, and I found myself smiling in return. I'd missed making him laugh and hearing his warm, hearty chuckles.

I gently led Rascal away from the pretzel cart. The three of us walked over to the next street, and I peppered him with more questions.

"What about your speed power? Have you always had it? What was the one thing that made you decide to be a hero?"

Kyle shrugged. "I've always had my power, ever since I can remember. I was just born with it. As for what made me actually decide to suit up and become a hero, it was a villain named Bustling Blue."

My heart squeezed tight, and I stumbled forward, almost stepping on Rascal, who let out a sharp, reproachful bark. Kyle slid up next to me and took hold of my elbow, his movements almost too fast for me to follow.

"Are you okay?" he asked, helping me to steady myself.

I forced myself to smile and move away from him. "Just a little clumsy. That's all."

Kyle looked at me another moment, making sure that I was okay, then we started walking again.

"So have you heard of him?" Kyle asked. "Bustling Blue? He has a speed power, like me. If anyone would know about him, it would be you, Piper."

"Yeah," I said in a faint voice. "I've heard of him."

I had met Blue after we had broken up, so Kyle had no idea that I knew the former villain. He must not have seen the news about Blue's murder yet. Otherwise, his tone would have been much, much different.

I swallowed down the sadness clogging my throat. "So what did Blue have to do with you?"

"Believe it or not, I was a total brat when I was a kid," Kyle said, grinning. "Once I figured out how to use my power, I started messing with people. Picking pockets, stealing watches off people's wrists, snatching their food and drinks before they could eat them."

"Until..."

"Until one day, when I swiped this guy's wad of cotton candy in Paradise Park. He was in costume so I knew that he had some sort of power, but I didn't care who he was or what he could do. Even though I wasn't all that swift back then, I was a stupid, arrogant kid, so I didn't think that anyone else was as fast as me. I didn't expect the guy to run after and catch up to me, but he did, and it was Bustling Blue."

Kyle stared off into the distance, his eyes soft with memories. "He gave me a good, stern talking-to and told me that if I could run that fast as a kid, then I might as well grow up, be a good guy, and use my speed to help people." He grinned. "And that if he ever saw me stealing cotton candy again, he'd make me eat cones and cones of it until I was sick of the stuff."

He laughed at the memory. "Good ole Bustling Blue. I wonder what ever happened to him?"

My stomach twisted. I didn't have the heart to tell him. Not yet. Let him enjoy his happy recollections at least a few minutes longer.

We turned the corner and reached one of the entrances to Paradise Park, which was one of Bigtime's most popular attractions. The park was open twenty-four hours a day, year-round, and featured all sorts of rides, carnival games, food carts, and more. Cheery calliope music trilled through the air, and the scents of funnel cakes and other fried foods made my stomach rumble, despite the hearty lunch I'd just eaten at Quicke's. Maybe Fiona was rubbing off on me.

Kyle stepped onto a cobblestone path, and we went deep into the park, eventually wandering through an area filled with marble fountains spewing water up into the air. Given the clouds of chilly mist that hung in the air, this section of the park was deserted, except for a single Snowdom truck parked on a nearby access road. But the truck was dark and closed up tight. I guess nobody wanted ice cream when it was this cold outside.

We walked to the far side of the fountain area. In the distance, wooden booths covered with bright, glittery signs had been set up on one of the park's many snow-covered lawns. Kids and their parents were already lined up, eager to meet their favorite heroes, and I spotted a woman wearing a khaki fisherman's vest going from booth to booth, checking things off on a clipboard. Chloe Cavanaugh, Abby's event-planning partner, who was handling things while Abby was on vacation with Wesley.

Kyle stopped and looked around. But the fountain area was deserted, so he felt safe enough to lift his mask up onto his head, revealing his face to me again.

Rascal started sniffing around the fountains, so I put my purse down on a nearby bench and tied his leash to one of the iron slats so that he could explore a little bit but not wander off too far.

Kyle crossed his arms over his chest, and we faced each other.

"What's wrong, Piper?" he asked again. "Why all the questions? Is this about last night? And our…talk?"

"Yes, but it's not what you're thinking. Something happened to me after I saw you, on the way back to my apartment." I swallowed again, dreading what I had to tell him now. "It has to do with the guy you mentioned. Bustling Blue. He had been hanging around Fiona's store, and I had gotten to know him over the past few months…"

I blinked back the tears that had gathered in my eyes, drew in a breath, and told him about finding Blue's body and all the things he'd said before he'd died, all the warnings he'd given me. I also told Kyle what Fiona had said about the fabric scrap and color being a match for Frost's costume.

Kyle's jaw clenched tight, his hands curled into fists, and he started pacing back and forth in front of me. Emotions flashed in his eyes almost as fast as he could run. Shock. Disbelief. Disgust. Anger.

Yeah. That's how I felt too, every time I thought about what Frost had done to Blue.

"Poor Blue." Kyle stopped pacing and shook his head. "Having your blood, your powers drained out of you... It's every hero's and villain's worst fear. He didn't deserve that."

"No, he didn't," I said in a quiet voice. "He didn't deserve any of it. Neither did the other people that Frost murdered."

Kyle frowned. "Are you sure that Frost is behind all this? And not some copycat villain? Because he's been missing for more than a year now. Nobody's seen him since Karma Girl and the rest of the Fearless Five blew up the old Snowdom Ice Cream Factory while he, Malefica, and Scorpion were inside. No one's heard anything from Frost or the other two villains since then."

I shrugged. "I suppose it could be a copycat. I don't know. But I was worried about you, and I wanted to come and warn you in person."

"Thanks for the heads-up. I appreciate it. But you don't have to worry about me. I'll be on guard now."

Kyle nodded and started to walk past me, but I stepped in front of him.

"Can we talk?" I asked. "Really talk? Finally try to figure out things between us? Please?"

"There's nothing to talk about."

"Yes, there is," I insisted. "Because I still love you. I've never stopped loving you."

He dropped his head and leaned forward, like he was going to slam his mask back down over his face and race away from me as fast as he could, just like he had last night. But this time, I was ready for the move. I stepped up and grabbed his gloved hand, clasping it in both of mine and raising it up so that it rested against my heart, which was beating hard and fast.

Kyle looked at me, but for the first time in months, he didn't pull away, and I almost thought I saw a bit of wary hope spark to life in his blue eyes. Or maybe that was just wishful thinking on my part. Either way, I hurried on, getting the words out as fast as I could.

"I was an idiot, going on and on about Swifte the way I did," I said. "But I was hoping you would open up and share your secret identity with me. That's all I was trying to do."

He shook his head again. "I wish you didn't know that I was him. I wish I could be sure that you loved *me*, and not just the idea of me as a superhero."

"I don't love you because you're Swifte—I love Swifte because he's a part of *you*."

Kyle sighed. "That may be true, but what happens when I can't be Swifte anymore? When I get old and wrinkled and worn-out, like Blue?"

"Then I'll love you even more," I said. "Because I'll be old and wrinkled and worn-out right there with you. We'll sit on the front porch of our house in our rocking chairs, and you can tell our young, whippersnapper grandkids all about how cool it was to be the fastest superhero in Bigtime."

He stared at me, that wary hope burning a little brighter and warring with all his fears and insecurities. He was wavering, thinking about my words, actually hearing them more than he ever had before.

"Please, Kyle," I said in a soft voice. "Give me a second chance. Give *us* a second chance. Let me prove how much I love *you*, Kyle Quicke. That's all I want. That's all I've wanted for months now."

He stared at me, still, silent, and stoic. As far away as ever before, even though he was standing right in front of me.

"At least tell me one thing then," I said, trying a different tactic.

"What?"

"After we broke up, why didn't you get Mr. Sage to mindwipe me like you did all the other people who discovered your secret identity?"

He blinked, as if surprised by the question. "I don't know," he said in a low voice. "I guess that...I thought that...you deserved to know. And to keep on knowing. About me and Swifte and why I had to end things between us. I didn't want you to think that I had hurt you for no reason, and that's what would have happened if Mr. Sage had mindwiped you. You would have hated me, and I...I just couldn't stand that."

"But why trust me to keep your real identity a secret? Why me, out of all the people who've found out over the years? Why take the risk?"

The corner of his mouth lifted up into a wry smile. "I've always trusted you, Piper. More than anyone else I've ever met. Besides, I know *you*, remember? You would never reveal a hero's real identity. You know how much danger it would put the hero in, not to mention his friends and family."

He was right. Those were some of the many reasons why I didn't shout everyone's real identities from the rooftops. The heroes had these colorful, code-named personas to protect themselves and their families from ubervillains and the like, and I respected that. I didn't even tell Abby, my best friend, about who was who, and I hadn't said a word to her about Kyle being Swifte or why we'd really broken up.

Still, Kyle's words touched me more than he knew. Because even though we weren't together anymore, he had trusted me with his most precious secret for all these months. Hope flared to life in my heart. He wouldn't have done that if he didn't still care about me, if he didn't think there was still a chance for us.

More and more feelings, more and more words bubbled up in my chest, and for once, I let them all out, laid it all on the line, laid myself and my heart right out there in the open for him to see.

"Even if you tell me no, even if you push me away right now, I'm not going to give up on us. Never again. I'm going to keep telling you how much I love you until you finally believe it. No matter how long it takes." I grinned. "Who knows? Maybe being stubborn is my own personal superpower."

Kyle kept staring and staring at me, so I moved even closer to him, looking up into his eyes. He didn't pull back, and he didn't race away like he had so many times before. So I took another chance. I wrapped my arms around his neck, pulled his face down to mine, and planted a soft kiss on his lips.

Nothing happened.

Kyle just stood there, not making any effort to kiss me back and not showing any signs that he wanted to do so ever again. Hurt welled up inside me, but I kept right on kissing him, pouring all the love, all the passion, all the feeling that I had for him into this one desperate kiss.

And still, nothing happened.

More hurt flooded my heart, and my cheeks burned with embarrassment. Disappointed, I broke off the kiss and started to pull back—

WHOOSH!

In an instant, Kyle gathered me up in his arms, slammed his lips back down onto mine, and kissed me and kissed me and kissed me some more.

Heat roared through my veins, chasing away the chill from the fountains' mist and the brisk winter air. I sighed and melted into his embrace, threading my fingers through his silky hair, even as my tongue danced against his. In an instant, my heart felt lighter than it had since the night of our breakup. We were together again, now, here, in this moment, and I was determined that this wasn't going to be the last kiss, the last touch, the last bit of happiness between us. It would take some time, but Kyle and I could get back on track—together. I *knew* that we could, and I was going to do everything in my power to make it happen.

Rascal started whining, then growling, but I tuned out the puppy, so caught up in the feel of Kyle's lips on mine, his hands cupping my face, his body pressed up against mine, that nothing else mattered.

I don't know how long we stood there kissing, with the fountains' mist washing over us in cold waves and the calliope music blaring in the distance, but we finally, slowly, reluctantly broke apart, both of us panting, our breaths mixing, mingling, and frosting together in the winter air.

Kyle leaned down and rested his forehead on mine. I tightened my grip on his shoulders, not wanting him to speed off and disappear on me like he had so many times before.

"Does this mean that you finally forgive me?" I asked in a husky voice.

"There's nothing to forgive," he whispered back. "I'm sorry for being such an insecure idiot."

I tilted my head back and grinned at him. "I *might* be able to forgive you for that."

He cocked an eyebrow. "If..."

"If you kiss me like that again. Right here, right now." My grin widened. "And then later on tonight, when we're alone together in my apartment."

Kyle grinned back and leaned in, his hot gaze dropping to my lips again. "Oh, I think I can manage that..."

Rascal let out a bark, followed by a low, angry growl, but all I was focused on was Kyle and his lips inching closer to mine—

"How very touching," a snide voice called out.

Kyle and I jerked apart to find a man standing a few feet away.

He was a thin guy, even leaner than Kyle was. So thin that he looked like he had been sick for quite some time. His hair was so light and blond that it was almost white, although his eyes were a bright, piercing, almost neon-blue behind his mask, one with distinctive, icicle-shaped edges. I'd never seen him in person before, but he looked different than in all the photos I remembered. He was not only painfully thin but he had long, red, jagged scars marring what I could see of his face outside his mask, as though an animal—or more than one—had clawed and clawed at him.

According to the rumors I'd heard, he had been attacked by the animals he'd been experimenting on when Karma Girl and the Fearless Five had defeated him. That would certainly explain the red, vivid scars that stood out against his pale skin like puckered, bloody scratches. But what chilled me to the bone was the ice-blue costume he wore—ice-blue forty-two, to be precise.

Frost.

One of the most feared ubervillains to ever haunt the streets of Bigtime. Here. In the park. With Kyle and me. With Kyle wearing his costume but not his mask. And having just heard me talk all about Kyle's secret identity as Swifte.

Frost was holding a complicated-looking gun bristling with all sorts of buttons—the same freezoray gun I'd seen him use in countless news stories and live SNN feeds from battle sites.

The same gun he had leveled at my heart right now.

I blinked. From one second to the next, Kyle moved so that he was standing in front of me, protecting me from the ubervillain. Rascal was still growling and straining at the end of his leash, which was tied to the park bench, but the puppy wasn't anywhere close to Frost. Good. That was good.

Kyle pulled his mask back down, covering his face and morphing into the superhero that I knew and loved so well.

"Frost, man, long time, no see," Swifte drawled. "I wish you had kept it that way."

Frost shrugged.

"Where have you been all this time?" Swifte asked, taking a step forward, his hands clenching into fists, his gaze locked onto the freezoray gun, waiting for a chance to take down the ubervillain.

Frost shrugged again. "After Malefica's debacle with Karma Girl, I spent several months recovering. Since then, I've been laying low and focusing on my experiments. Perfecting some new projects that I had been thinking about for quite some time."

Anger burned in my heart. My hands clenched into fists, and I stepped up beside Swifte. "Like murdering people and stealing their superpowers?"

For the first time, Frost deigned to look at me, although his blue eyes were cold and completely empty, as though I were a bug that was far, far beneath his notice.

"Well, you don't have to worry about that, since you have no powers worth stealing. In fact, you don't have any powers at all, do you, Ms. Perez?"

My blood chilled a little more. "How do you know my name?"

Frost smirked at me. "Did you know that you've been featured on SNN quite a few times? It seems like you're *always* getting yourself into some sort of trouble that some idiot superhero has to come and bail you out of. SNN had quite a good shot of Swifte here embracing you after one of your fiascos a few months ago."

"The runaway bus," I whispered.

I'd been so shocked to discover that Kyle was really Swifte that I hadn't paid much attention to the SNN news coverage of the bus accident, although several folks in the *Slaves for Superhero Sex* club had texted to tell me congrats on locking lips with Swifte and had begged for all the juicy details. But Frost had been watching the coverage—and me too.

"That was what first got me interested in you, Ms. Perez,"

Frost said. "I'll admit that I was a bit bored during my recovery, so I started following you around as part of an experiment. I didn't think that it was statistically possible for someone to accidentally get into so much trouble, but you proved all my theories wrong. Quite fascinating, actually. Your repeated misfortunes almost make me believe that some things as silly as bad luck and karma actually exist."

"You've been following me around?" I asked. "Why?"

"Like I said, I was bored—at first. But then, you volunteered for that little library project and started chatting up all those old, nobody heroes and villains. I'd forgotten just how many heroes and villains there are in this town—and how many different powers they had that were worth taking."

"So you did kill Bustling Blue," I whispered. "And all the others. You murdered them for their powers."

And I had helped him do it.

I had painted a target on Blue's back and all those other folks just by talking to them. Just by being my idiot superfan self, seeking them out and wanting to hear their stories. I had never even thought about the possibility that someone might be following me—or what he might do with the knowledge of where all those retired superfolks were.

My heart squeezed tight with shock, guilt, and shame. Hot, queasy nausea boiled up in my stomach, and I had to fight back the urge to be sick on the spot.

"Of course I killed them," Frost sneered. "Those old farts weren't using their abilities anymore, so I took them. I did them a *favor*, putting them out of their misery. There's nothing sadder or more pathetic than a washed-up hero or villain. They were all just wasting away in those nursing homes or sitting inside their apartments, waiting to die. But I set them free, and I ensured that their powers would finally be put to good use."

"Give it up," Swifte said. "You're not stealing any more powers, and you're certainly not hurting anyone else."

Frost gave him an indulgent smile. "Ah, that's where you're wrong, Swifte. Then again, you aren't much of a thinker, are you? You always just rely on your motormouth and superspeed to get by. Well, I'm here to tell you that it won't be enough. Not this time. If you're lucky, maybe I'll let your little civilian girlfriend live."

Swifte stepped forward, his hands balling into tight fists. "Don't you dare say another word about Piper. You aren't hurting her or anyone else."

Frost rolled his eyes. "Superheroes. Always so dramatic. I've already won. You just don't know it yet."

Swifte darted forward, zooming toward Frost. In the blink of an eye, he was right in front of the ubervillain. Almost too quick for me to follow, Swifte snapped his hand forward, punching Frost in the jaw.

But instead of connecting, his hand passed right through the villain's face, like Frost wasn't even standing there.

Swifte stopped, as confused as I was.

Frost laughed. "While I've been gone, I've made some improvements to my freezoray gun," he purred. "Holograms are one of them. Now you see me…"

The image of him vanished, then reappeared a second later some twenty feet away.

"Now you see me again." He let out another loud, crazy, maniacal laugh.

Rascal kept growling and growling, but he wasn't looking at the hologram. Instead, the puppy was turned around in the opposite direction. I glanced over my shoulder and realized that there was another Frost standing behind us—and that his finger was curling back on the trigger of his freezoray gun.

"Swifte! Look out!" I screamed.

Swifte whipped around and started speeding toward Frost. Swifte was quick, but so was Frost now, thanks to the speed power he'd stolen from Bustling Blue, and he was just fast enough to pull the trigger on his gun right before Swifte reached him.

An ice-blue ray shot out from the end of the barrel and hit Swifte square in the chest. The blast knocked him back ten feet, and he hit the side of the park bench that Rascal was tied to and bounced off. He crumpled to the cobblestones, and he didn't move.

"Swifte!" I yelled, running toward him. "Swifte!"

Frost rolled his eyes again at my frantic screams, then waved his hand. An intense burst of light filled the area, so white, hot, and bright that it made me scream even louder. I slapped my hands over my eyes to block out the light, but the damage had already been done. Rascal whined too, his eyes getting burned just like mine were.

After several seconds, the light faded away, although white stars kept exploding over and over again in my field of vision, causing my head to ache, as though I had the worst migraine ever. I blinked and realized that Frost was standing right in front of me, a gloating sneer twisting his face and making him look even more horrific than his red, jagged scars did.

"Light pulses, courtesy of Catwalk," Frost said. "See? I told you that I was going to put those powers to good use. And with Swifte's superspeed, no one will be able to stop me from taking all the powers I want. And then Bigtime will be mine, the way it should have been all along."

My hands bunched into fists again, and I lunged for him, but Frost still had Bustling Blue's speed. He wasn't as fast as Swifte, but he still easily sidestepped me. I tripped and fell down onto my hands and knees. By the time I had scrambled up again, Frost already had Swifte slung over his shoulder in a fireman's carry and was striding away with him, heading toward the access road where that ice cream truck was parked. Of course he could carry Swifte away. The villain had Muscular Mila's strength to help him with that now.

"Kyle!" I screamed. "Kyle!"

Even as I started forward, I knew that I was going to be too slow, too weak, and too late. Frost sighed as if I were a fly, buzzing around his head and totally annoying him. He stopped, turned around, leveled his freezoray gun at me, and pulled the trigger.

That ice-blue light flashed again. I tried to throw myself to one side, but I wasn't quick enough. A blast of cold swept over me, colder than any chill I'd ever felt before, and the world went black.

PART THREE
FANDEMIC

Chapter Eight

Something warm, wet, and sticky touched my face, jolting me out of the cold blackness I'd been drifting along in.

I sucked in a breath and opened my eyes. Rascal was standing next to me, one tiny paw on my chest as though he'd been trying to shake me awake. He leaned in and licked my cheek again, his puppy chow breath making my nose wrinkle. I dug my fingers into his fur, then reached up and scratched his ears. He let out a soft whine and snuggled even closer to me.

"Good boy," I croaked. "Good boy."

I tried to sit up and groaned as an ache exploded in the back of my skull. Whatever was in Frost's freezoray gun packed a heck of a wallop. I wondered if it was some sort of radioactive chemical. I'd have to do some research on that. Maybe Kyle could tell me. He'd been hit by the gun before—

Kyle! Frost had Kyle!

Everything came rushing back to me, and I sat bolt upright. I even tried to get up onto my feet, but my headache intensified, my legs slid out from under me, and I ended up falling back down onto my ass on the cold, wet pavement. I groaned again and cradled my head in my hands, trying to push the pain away.

I didn't have time to be hurt or weak right now. I had to find Kyle. I had to save him from Frost. No matter what.

So I forced myself to lift my head again. The world spun around and around for several seconds, but I concentrated, and the dizzying rush slowly faded away. I blinked and realized that I was staring at that access road that wrapped around the fountain area. The old, battered ice cream truck that had been parked there earlier was long gone. I cursed. Of course it was.

"Hey, Piper," a concerned voice called out. "Are you okay? You look a little pale. And cold. Yeah, pale and cold."

Something *tap-tap-tapped*, getting louder and louder the closer it got to me. I must have still been kind of out of it because I blinked, and suddenly, a cane was planted on the cobblestones next to me. I looked up to find a woman standing over me, wearing a very nice Bulluci fleece pullover with a messenger bag slung across her chest. Concern filled her dark eyes, while the weak winter sun made the neon-blue streaks in her black hair shimmer.

"Lulu?" I asked. "What are you doing here?"

"The one and only." Lulu Lo grinned and waved her hand in an elaborate flourish. "Um, Piper, what are you doing out here all by yourself? Did you get mugged or something?"

I groaned. "You could say that."

Lulu reached down and helped me up onto my feet. I was still a bit unsteady, and my legs wobbled like they were made out of melting ice, but at least I was upright again. I'd gotten lucky. Frost could have easily set his gun to kill instead of merely stun.

"Piper?" Lulu asked again. "What happened? What's wrong?"

"Frost has Kyle, er, Swifte," I mumbled through my cold, chapped lips. "Frost is the one who's been going around town stealing powers and murdering people. We have to find him. We have to save Swifte!"

I took a step forward and would have fallen face-first onto the cobblestones if Lulu hadn't reached out and steadied me.

"Whoa, there, tiger," she said, holding on to me until I was stable enough to stand on my own again. "Take it easy."

"I can't take it easy. Not until I know that Swifte is okay." I grabbed her. "You! Lulu! You have to help me save him!"

My hands fisted in the soft fabric of her fleece pullover. Lulu pried my fingers loose and slowly backed away from me.

"Whoa, there," she repeated. "I think you've been hit in the head a little too hard. You're talking crazy. Besides, *we* don't have to do anything. All I have to do is call the Fearless Five, and they'll take care of the rest. You'll see."

Lulu whipped out her smartphone and hit a number in the speed dial. I paced back and forth in front of her, waiting for someone to answer. Rascal whined at my feet, picking up on my stress and tension. But even when Lulu connected with the superheroes, it would still take the Fearless Five precious time to reach Kyle, time that just might cost him his speedy superpower—and his life.

Lulu frowned and pulled her phone away from her ear. "That's weird."

My heart sank. "What's weird?"

"They're not answering. Let me try something else."

She hit several more buttons on her phone, probably texting Henry "Hermit" Harris, her fiancé. I whipped out my own phone and hit Fiona's number. It rang and rang before going to her voice mail.

"*Hi, you've reached Fiona Fine. Life is too short for boring fashion, so be as fabulous as possible. Leave me a message, darling, and I'll get back to you as soon as I can…*"

"Fiona," I growled after the beep. "Pick up your damn phone. This is an *emergency*. I just saw Frost in Paradise Park. He kidnapped Swifte and is probably going to take his speed power before he kills him. Call me back as soon as you get this."

I hung up to find Lulu staring at me, her dark eyes narrowed.

"What?" I growled again.

"You called *Fiona Fine* to help you with a superhero problem," she asked. "Why would you do that, Piper?"

Normally, I would have done my whole blank smile and song-and-dance routine and made up some lame excuse, but there was no time. Not when Kyle was in danger.

I threw my hands up in exasperation. "Because she's really Fiera, that's why! You know, if people in this city want to have secret identities, then they shouldn't make them so easy to figure out and so bloody obvious who they really are. Now should they?"

I slapped my hands on my hips and glared at Lulu. She held her own hands up in mock surrender and backed away from me.

"Take it easy there, tiger," she repeated. "I was just asking. Although...how do you know about Fiona?"

I rolled my eyes. "Please. How else could she eat so much and not weigh a ton if she didn't have a high metabolism and some sort of superpower?"

Lulu nodded. "Good point."

"Now where are they?" I asked. "What is so important that the Fearless Five aren't answering their phones and help hotline?"

Lulu waved her phone at me. "Big pileup on the interstate. More than a hundred cars involved, trucks overturned, fires spreading from vehicle to vehicle, gas and chemicals and radioactive goo leaking everywhere. The Fearless Five are helping to clean up the mess." She hesitated. "It'll probably be hours before they even think to check the hotline or any of their phones. I'm sorry, Piper."

I rubbed my temples, which were still throbbing. "Well, Kyle, er, Swifte doesn't have hours. He'll be dead by the time the Fearless Five get around to helping him."

And I couldn't call Wesley "Talon" Weston to help either, since he and Abby were on vacation and out of town. Frustration surged through me, and I started pacing back and forth again.

The Fearless Five were busy, and Talon was gone. So who else was out there? Who else could I get to help me save Kyle?

A thought occurred to me, and I stopped in my tracks. "What other heroes are helping the Fearless Five with the interstate crash?"

Lulu scrolled through some screens on her phone. "According to the SNN news feed, Halitosis Hal, Pistol Pete, Johnny Angel, and the Invisbile Ingénues are all helping out as best they can. Debonair is there too, teleporting people out of their crashed cars."

She held the device out to me. Sure enough, Kelly Caleb was already reporting from the scene of the horrible accident, giving update after update as the camera panned over the interstate. Crashed cars, overturned trucks, fires. It looked even worse than Lulu's description, but I focused on the heroes running around and moving people away from the twisted, crumpled, burning wreckage. Halitosis Hal, Pistol Pete, Johnny Angel, the Invisbile Ingénues... I spotted all the heroes that Lulu had mentioned, along with the Fearless Five, but there was one hero who I didn't see.

"All right," I said. "Thanks for your help. I'll take it from here."

Lulu stared at me. "What are you going to do, Piper?"

I squared my shoulders. "I'm going to save a superhero—*my* superhero."

I untied Rascal's leash from the bench, grabbed my purse, and marched out of Paradise Park, with the puppy trotting along beside me.

"Hey!" a voice called out. "Wait up!"

I turned to find Lulu leaning on her cane and walking up behind me. "What are you doing?"

She grinned. "I'm coming with you."

I shook my head. "I can't ask you to do that. It's too dangerous. Swifte is my, um, friend. I should be the one to rescue him."

Lulu gave me a knowing look. "Swifte is really Kyle Quicke, isn't he? That's why you're so hot and bothered that Frost has him."

I blinked. "How do you know that?"

She shrugged. "I remember you two dating last year. And every time I've seen you together in the same room since then, you've both spent the whole time shooting mopey looks at each other. Besides, you kept calling him *Kyle* while we were talking. *Total* giveaway."

I opened my mouth to deny that Kyle was really Swifte, but I clamped my lips together. There was no point in denying it. Not now when his life was at stake. If I rescued him from Frost—*when* I rescued him from Frost—we could worry about swearing Lulu to secrecy. But for now, time was the most important thing.

Besides, Lulu also had a friend who might be able to help me—even if he didn't know it yet.

"I know that you're worried sick about Kyle, but you're going to need some help, Piper," Lulu said in a soft voice. "Frost isn't a villain you want to mess around with. Even the people in the *Slaves for Superhero Sex* club steer clear of him. And you know how crazy those folks are."

I winced, since I was one of those crazy folks too, but she was right.

"Okay," I said. "Message received. Thank you."

Lulu nodded. "Now, what are we going to do?"

"First things first. We're going shopping."

Lulu and I walked to the edge of Paradise Park, along with Rascal, then hopped into a cab. A few minutes later, the cab stopped in front of the entrance to Oodles o' Stuff, Bigtime's preeminent department store.

I paid the cabbie, then marched inside the store and grabbed the biggest shopping cart I could find. I checked the map by the entrance that showed the layout of the store, all the various departments and items, and which floor they were located on.

"We'll start at the top and work our way down," I told Lulu. "Follow me."

I picked up Rascal and put him in the front of the cart so I wouldn't lose track of him. Then I rolled the cart over to the nearest elevator and got in. It was a tight fit with me, my jumbo cart, and Lulu, but we managed it. A minute later, the elevator opened on the top floor, and I headed over to one of the accessories counters and started browsing through the racks of sunglasses.

Lulu slowly came up behind me. "Um, Piper? I hate to be…critical, but do you think *now* is really the best time to shop for sunglasses? You know, when one of the worst ubervillains in the history of Bigtime has taken your one true love hostage and stuff?"

I dropped three pairs of sunglasses into the cart, along with a set of doggie goggles for Rascal. "I think it's the *perfect* time to get sunglasses. We're going to need some other stuff too. Do you think they have bullhorns here? Surely, they do. This is Oodles. They have *everything*."

Lulu gave me a look that clearly said she thought that I had lost my mind, but she followed along behind me. We went from one part of the store and one floor to the next, and I piled my cart high with all sorts of odd things—a bullhorn, khaki fishermen's vests, flashlights, a miniature heater, those chemical packs that warm you up when you rip them open and stick them in your pockets.

While I shopped, Lulu pulled out her phone and started tapping and scrolling away on it, alternating between trying to contact the Fearless Five and trying figure out where Frost might have taken Kyle. I had my own suspicions about that, but I let her keep searching, in case she found out something different. Rascal kept leaning out of the cart and sniffing her phone.

"So far, I've got nothing," she muttered, absently scratching the puppy's head to keep him from licking her phone screen again. "Apparently, Frost is being a little more careful about hiding his supersecret lab than he was the last time when Carmen found it—"

She stopped and gave me a guilty look.

"When Carmen Cole went to rescue the Fearless Five, got dropped into a vat of radioactive goo, developed superpowers, and became Karma Girl." I shook my head. "Some girls have all the luck."

Lulu gave me another *you're-a-little-no-scratch-that-a-whole-lot-crazy* look. "If you say so, Piper."

"I say so," I replied. "Now, let's go get the last thing we need."

Lulu looked over the items in my cart. "And what would that be?"

I grinned. "Why, a superhero, of course."

Chapter Nine

Lulu, Rascal, and I got back into the elevator and rode down to the ground floor. Lulu stepped out first, with me pushing the cart and Rascal, who was still riding up in the front of it, following along behind her.

"Where to?" Lulu asked.

"The makeup counter."

She gave me another disbelieving look, but she headed in that direction. We maneuvered around the other shoppers and made it to the middle of the first floor of Oodles o' Stuff. Glass counters full of every conceivable kind and color of makeup spiraled out in circles in this part of the store, along with counters filled with perfume bottles.

The overpowering mix of scents made my allergies flare up like firecrackers. I sneezed violently a couple of times and had to fish around in my purse for some tissues, which I sneezed into several more times. I finished with the tissues, looked up, and realized that I was standing next to a cardboard figure of Swifte, designed to display his latest cologne for men, *Eau de Swifte*. My heart squeezed, and I forced myself to push the cart on past his smiling face.

I stalked through the aisles until I finally found what—or rather who—I was looking for.

Sabrina St. John stood behind one of the Glo-Glo makeup counters, taking inventory of the items inside and marking them off on a clipboard sitting on the glass in front of her. She was dressed in a pale blue pantsuit, and her short, cropped blond hair gleamed underneath the store's lights. She looked up at the steady *squeak-squeak-squeak* of my shopping cart, and her face creased into a wary, thoughtful frown at the sight of me. I wondered if she had as hard a time remembering who knew what about whose secret identity as I did.

"Hi, Piper," Sabrina said in a guarded tone. "How are you?"

"Not good. Frost has kidnapped Swifte, and we need you to come with us." I gestured at myself and Lulu.

Rascal barked, chiding me for forgetting him.

Sabrina's blue eyes narrowed. "Frost has Swifte? Are you sure?"

"I was there. I'm sure. Now, come on. We still have another stop to make before we go over to the ice cream factory."

Lulu looked at me in surprise. I hadn't told her that was where we were ultimately headed.

Sabrina's frown deepened. "And why would I go with you to an ice cream factory?"

I sighed. "Because that's where Frost's secret lair is. Because you're really Wynter, and because you're one of the few heroes who aren't out helping with that pileup on the interstate right now. That's why."

Sabrina blinked and blinked for several seconds, the wheels turning in her mind as she debated whether or not to deny it. Finally, she sighed. "And exactly how did you figure out my secret identity?"

I shrugged. "I saw you change into your costume in one of the dressing rooms a few months ago."

"Snowballs!" she cursed. "I *knew* somebody saw me that day. I knew it! I just never thought it was you." Her eyes cut to Lulu. "Who's your friend?"

Lulu bowed. "Lulu Lo, at your superhero service."

Sabrina studied Lulu a moment, then her gaze dropped to the piles of merchandise in my shopping cart. "And what is all of *that?*"

"Supplies," I said. "If you're going to hunt an ubervillain who's amassed a bunch of superpowers, you really should be prepared, don't you think?"

"With sunglasses? And a bullhorn?" She frowned and stared at Lulu, who shrugged as if to say, *I don't know what the crazy chick is up to either.*

"Trust me. You will thank me for those sunglasses before this is all over with. Now are you in or not?"

Sabrina looked at me, then Lulu, then back at me. Rascal let out a small, hopeful bark. Sabrina stared at him too, along with all the odd items in my cart.

Her lips slowly curved up into a smile. "I'm always ready to kick a little ubervillain ass," she said. "Let's go."

Sabrina grabbed her purse while I paid for all the items in my cart, and we all met back at the front of the store. Even though I had almost a dozen bags, Sabrina just kept looping them on her arm one after another.

"Um, isn't all that a little heavy?" Lulu asked.

Sabrina held up her arm and made a classic flexing motion with her bicep. "Superstrength, remember?"

"Oh, yeah," Lulu said. "I forgot that you have all the same powers that Fiera does. Except for, you know, the fire."

Sabrina sniffed. "Please. Ice is *so* much better than fire. Far less destructive. At least when I take out a villain, I don't have to worry about setting every single thing in the immediate vicinity on fire. Did you see that four-alarm blaze Fiera started right outside the hospital last week?" She shook her head. "And she calls herself a superhero."

Lulu and I exchanged a look, and Lulu rolled her eyes. Yeah, me too. Sometimes, I thought that the heroes had more rivalries with each other than they did with their arch-nemesis villains.

The three of us, along with Rascal, went outside and hailed a cab. Lulu told the cabbie to take us back to Paradise Park, where her van was parked. We got there and piled inside her vehicle.

Lulu slid behind the wheel. "Now where to?"

I rattled off an address.

Her dark eyes widened, and the blue streaks in her hair seemed to spike up with shock. "How do you know about *him?*"

I shrugged. "I just know things. Besides, he lives across the street from Abby, my best friend, remember?"

"He's not going to like this. Another person knowing who he is and what he makes in his basement."

"I don't care if he likes it, as long as he helps us."

Lulu shook her head. "It's your funeral, Piper."

She drove her van over to Abby's street and stopped in front of the brownstone. Lulu, Sabrina, and I went up to the front door, with Rascal trotting along beside me. I rang the buzzer, and a security camera mounted over the entrance swiveled around to focus on me.

"The word is—" Lulu started, as though she were going to say some kind of password.

"I don't care what the word is," I growled, staring up at the camera. "Frost has kidnapped Swifte. So you know why I'm here and what I want. So open the door. Please."

Several seconds passed. Worry filled my stomach like a lead weight, and I held my breath, wondering if he'd really agree to help me, since I was more or less a complete stranger and the furthest thing from a superhero. But the door finally buzzed open. I stepped forward and opened it before he could change his mind, and we walked inside.

I'd never been inside Jasper's brownstone before, but what I could see of it from the entryway looked surprisingly nice and normal, with spacious rooms filled with lots of bookcases. Jasper stood a few feet inside the door, wearing his glasses and another pair of gray coveralls, his arms crossed over his chest.

He looked at me a moment, then Sabrina, before fixing his violet gaze on Lulu. "Do I even have to ask how much of the city you're going to destroy this time?"

Lulu grinned and went over to him, and the two of them did a complicated handshake. "Aw, c'mon, Jasper. You know you love to help a girl out. Or rather, help us blow stuff up."

"First, Carmen. Then Fiera and Bella. And now this." He sighed and shook his head. "Sometimes, I think you and your friends are going to be the death of me, Lulu. Or at least get me a one-way ticket to the state pen."

She held up her hands. "Hey, this wasn't my idea. It was all Piper's. She's the one who already knew all about your sideline business, and she needs your help. Tell him, Piper."

I explained how Frost had kidnapped Swifte, that most of the other superheroes were busy with the interstate pileup, and that the three of us were the only ones who had a chance of rescuing Kyle before Frost sucked out his blood and powers and murdered him.

When I finished, Jasper nodded. "Okay, okay. Swifte has helped me in the past, and any friend of Lulu's is a friend of mine." He paused and narrowed his eyes. "As long as you have enough cash for this sort of thing."

I opened my purse, dug through my wallet, and handed him a credit card. "I have something even better. A Fiona Fine Fashions corporate account. Just put it all on that."

Lulu let out a low whistle. "And what will Fiona say when she gets the bill?"

I shrugged. "She'll probably just set something on fire. You know how she is. But I'll soften her up with lunch from Quicke's. And doughnuts from Bryn's Bakery. And food from pretty much every other restaurant in the greater Bigtime area. Times two."

"And you know how she is too," Lulu warned. "Better make that times three."

I considered it. "Yeah, you're right. Times three it is."

Jasper led us down to his basement workshop and pulled out several solidium cases, all of which were lined with black foam and contained a variety of explosives, some of which were even shaped like pineapples. Weird.

"Do you have anything smaller?" I asked. "Like, just for blowing locks?"

He blinked. "You mean you don't want to level some building on top of Frost's head and bury him once and for all?"

I shrugged. "I want to rescue Swifte. I don't care what happens to Frost after that."

That wasn't entirely true, since the ubervillain had used me to murder innocent people. Rage still boiled in my heart when I thought about that, but I forced myself to smother that emotion with cold reason. This was a rescue, not a suicide mission, and I didn't want to blow up myself or the others in the process of saving Swifte. Kyle would never forgive me if I got myself killed, especially when we were finally trying to set things right between us again.

So Jasper pulled out another case, which featured much smaller bombs that were shaped like cherries, complete with the stems. He said that these were new, weaker versions of some of his older bomb designs, showed me how to use them by pulling the stems out of the cherries, then made me repeat the steps back to him. Lulu and Sabrina watched as well. When he was satisfied that all three of us knew what we were doing with the explosives, Jasper closed the case, handed it over to me, and sent us on our way.

We went out to the van, and Sabrina climbed into the back. I don't know exactly how she managed it, given all the computer equipment that Lulu had crammed into the vehicle, but Sabrina stripped off her clothes, pulled her Wynter costume and mask out of her oversize purse, and shimmied into them in less than a minute. Rascal barked, wondering at the change in her. She climbed back into her seat, and I turned around and stared at her costume.

"Ice-blue fifty-one?" I asked.

"Good eye," Sabrina, Wynter, said. "How did you know?"

"Fiona gave me a very detailed lesson all about the various shades of ice-blue." I shuddered. "I know more about that color than I ever, *ever* wanted to. But enough about that. We have a superhero to save and an ubervillain to take down."

Lulu grinned. "I thought you'd never ask."

She cranked the van's engine and peeled away from the curb.

CHAPTER TEN

Thirty minutes later, Lulu pulled off the road and eased the van into a small wooded area. The sun was almost gone for the day, and darkness was creeping over everything. Through the trees, about two hundred feet ahead, lay what remained of the Snowdom Ice Cream Factory. Which was mostly a giant pile of rocky, ruined rubble.

Wynter peered through the windshield and frowned. "Are you sure this is where Frost is hiding out? It doesn't look like much, Piper."

"I'm sure."

Wynter and Lulu exchanged a look.

"And how do you know this, exactly?" Lulu asked. "Not that we're doubting you…except that we totally are right now."

I glared at her, but she shrugged back at me.

"Last night, when I found Blue in the alley outside the fashion store, there was an ice cream truck parked at the curb. I didn't think much of it at the time, especially since the truck was gone by the time the cops showed up. But I saw another ice cream truck by the fountains in the park today, almost as if someone had parked it there and was lurking inside, waiting for some superhero to walk by on their way over to that meet-and-greet event so he could kidnap them. When I woke up after Frost zapped me, that truck was gone. But it was the same truck I saw last night because it had the same exact lettering on the side. Care to guess what that lettering said?"

"Um, Snowdom Ice Cream Factory?" It wasn't really a guess on Lulu's part.

"Exactly." I pointed out the windshield. "And I see that same truck parked right over there next to what's left of the factory. Now why would there be a truck way out here if no one was around to drive it? And who else besides Frost would be driving it if this wasn't where his supersecret lair was?"

"True," Lulu agreed. "And who else would hole up in an abandoned ice cream factory that has been blown to bits other than a villain who'd been here before?"

"No one would even think to look for Frost way out here because the lair was already destroyed once before," Wynter chimed in. "Or so everyone thought."

Rascal barked his agreement as well. It made perfect sense— in a twisted, ubervillain sort of way.

"C'mon," I said. "Let's just hope we're not too late to save Kyle."

We got out of the van and sorted through all the supplies I'd bought. I handed Lulu one of the khaki mesh vests that I'd purchased at Oodles o' Stuff.

Lulu took it from me and held it out at arm's length, eyeing the vest with obvious disdain. She frowned. "Wait a second. Doesn't Abby always wear one of these?"

"Yep. And I am never making fun of her for that ever again. Now put it on and grab the rest of your gear."

Lulu grumbled some more, but she slipped on the vest and zipped it up. I did the same to mine. Wynter, of course, was in her costume and decided not to use a vest, although she did take the pair of sunglasses I gave her.

As a final touch, Lulu gave us each a set of earplugs from the stash of equipment in her van. Not only did the earplugs automatically adjust to let us hear what was happening around us, as well as block out loud, unexpected noises, but they also served as earwigs that let us communicate back and forth with each other.

"Nice," Wynter purred, her sultry voice echoing in my ear. "If I had a partner in crime, I would totally get you to make us some of these."

Lulu gave a little bow. "I am at your command, my lady."

Wynter snickered.

"If you two are done talking about how awesome you both are, maybe we can try to find Kyle before Frost kills him?" I asked in a snide tone.

That sobered up the two of them, and me as well. The whole ride over here, my heart had been twisting and twisting in my chest, like a dishrag that I couldn't wring all the fear and worry out of, no matter how hard I tried.

When we were all geared up, we left the van behind and slowly approached the rubble of the ice cream factory, heading toward the truck first. Wynter made Lulu and me hang back while she peered in the windows, then opened the side door.

"Empty," she called out.

I clicked on my flashlight and shined it around the interior of the truck. No blood. Good. That was good. That meant Kyle was most likely still alive. That was my hope anyway, and hope was all that I had to hang on to right now.

I started to turn away when something shimmered underneath my flashlight beam. "Wait. There's something in here."

I leaned forward, snagged something soft from a rusty bolt that was sticking up out of the truck floor, and held it up in my flashlight beam. A bit of opalescent white cloth glimmered in my hand. I turned and showed it to Lulu and Wynter.

"This is from Swifte's costume, which means that this is definitely Frost's truck," I said, slipping the cloth into one of the pockets on my vest. "They have to be around here somewhere. Let's go."

Wynter took the lead, and together, the three of us, plus Rascal, headed toward the rubble.

Carmen "Karma Girl" Cole had certainly done an impressive job of blowing the ice cream factory to smithereens. Oh, some of the exterior walls were still standing, but their tops were cut off, like blades of grass that had been whacked down as short as possible. The rest of the building had caved in on itself, and piles of rubble stretched out as far as I could see, with cracked support beams and jagged chunks of rebar sticking out of them like pins haphazardly poked into a cushion.

We moved slowly, picking our way through the debris, looking for some sort of path or trail leading deeper into the rubble, but we didn't find one. I didn't even see so much as a footprint in the dust and snow that had settled in and around the ruins.

"So how exactly are we going to find Frost's lab?" Lulu asked. "I don't know about you, but I don't have x-ray vision, and it's one of the few things they don't sell at Oodles o' Stuff."

"We don't need x-ray vision because we have someone here who has a supersense of smell." I looked down at Rascal. "Isn't that right, boy?"

The puppy let out an enthusiastic bark and wagged his tail, whipping up sprays of snow.

Wynter stared down at the puppy. "He's going to find Frost? Are you sure about that?"

"I'm sure. Rascal is a very smart, very special dog. Aren't you, boy?"

Rascal let out another enthusiastic bark as if to say, *You betcha!* Wynter still looked skeptical, though.

I didn't mention that Talon had already started training the puppy to be a search-and-rescue dog. That would require way too much explanation about how I knew Talon and how he was really Wesley Weston.

"And how is Rascal going to find the lab?" Lulu asked. "It's not like Frost put up signs to it or anything."

"Because Frost left something behind when he murdered Blue," I said. "This."

I reached into a pocket on my vest and fished out the scrap of ice-blue fabric I'd found in the alley last night. I just hoped there was enough of Frost's scent still left on it for Rascal to track the villain.

I crouched down and held the torn fabric out to the puppy. Rascal realized what I wanted and snapped to attention. He leaned in, his black nose quivering as he sniffed and sniffed every single bit of the fabric.

When he was finished, Rascal sat back on his heels, as if he were thinking. Maybe he was. Then he turned, put his nose to the ground, and started sniffing along it. I let out his leash as far as it would go and followed him, with Wynter and Lulu trailing along behind me.

It was slow going, given all the piles of rubble. Rascal was still so tiny and his legs were so short that he couldn't hurdle the biggest rocks, and I had to lift him up over them whenever he stopped and gave me a short, commanding bark.

The longer he sniffed and the deeper we moved into the factory ruins, the more my stomach filled with cold dread and heavy worry. It had seemed like a great plan at the time, using Rascal's nose to find Frost's lab. Now, I wondered whether I'd made the right choice—and whether I might have cost the man I loved his life.

"C'mon, boy," I murmured. "You can do it. I *know* you can."

If he didn't, Kyle was dead.

Rascal kept sniffing and sniffing, and we kept following him, deeper and deeper into the rubble until we'd reached the back side of what had once been the factory. Finally, just when I was about to give up all hope, the puppy stopped and started pawing at a patch of dirt. He looked up at me and let out another, louder bark as if to say, *Here he is!*

"Whatcha got, boy?" I asked, shining my flashlight over the spot where he was digging.

But all I saw were dirt, snow, and rocks—no doors, no tunnels, nothing that looked like an opening at all.

"I don't see anything," Lulu said, echoing my thoughts.

"There has to be some sort of secret entrance around here somewhere," I muttered. "We just have to find it. Frost does have Muscular Mila's strength now. Maybe he's lifting up a slab of concrete or something like that to get inside."

Wynter snorted. "I doubt that. Frost never was much for getting his hands dirty or exerting himself in any way."

"Help me look, guys," I said. "Please."

Wynter nodded, and the two of us stepped forward and stared out over the piles of rubble, while Lulu hung back. Rascal let out a sharp, reproachful yip, as though we should have already found the door he knew was here.

Lulu dusted some snow off a pile of rocks. Then she sat down, pulled her tablet out of her fisherman's vest, and started *tap-tap-tapping* on it, her fingers flying every which way across the screen.

"What are you doing?" I asked. "Put that away, and come help us search."

"You have your superpowers, and I have mine," she said. "Which includes hacking into the city's power grid. If Frost does have a lab here, then he has to have some kind of electricity running to it to fuel all of his uberevil gadgets. And electricity means power lines, which are a lot easier to find than secret doors."

Wynter and I stared at each other. The superhero shrugged and kept scanning the rubble. I did the same.

Lulu kept *tap-tap-tapping* on her tablet, murmuring to herself all the while about firewalls and encryptions and other things that I didn't understand. Finally, she looked up, as if orienting herself with the landscape, got to her feet, leaned on her cane, and took several steps forward.

"According to the city's electrical schematics, an underground power line runs through this section of the factory. Now, if I were a maniacal ubervillain who wanted to be all warm and toasty with plenty of lights and still have easy access to my lab, I think I would put a trapdoor or secret entrance right about...here."

Lulu poked her cane down into the dirt and snow.

Snick.

And just like that, a concrete slab rolled back, revealing a metal tunnel that sloped down into the ground.

Lulu grinned. "See? What did I tell you? These hands have superpowers too, baby."

She waggled her fingers at me and Wynter, then blew us both a kiss. Rascal cocked his head to the side, not understanding what she was doing. Wynter rolled her eyes, but I was just glad we'd discovered the lab entrance. It meant that we were one step closer to finding and rescuing Kyle.

If it wasn't already too late.

But I forced that chilling thought away. Kyle was alive—he *had* to be. I hadn't gotten him back just to lose him again, especially not to a villain like Frost.

So I tightened my grip on my flashlight and squared my shoulders. "Here we go," I whispered, then stepped down into the darkness.

CHAPTER ELEVEN

The slow, steady way the tunnel veered down into the ground reminded me of a ramp on the back of a cargo plane. We'd only gone about ten feet down when the concrete slab slid shut above our heads, leaving us in complete blackness, except for the glow from our flashlights.

"Now what?" Lulu muttered.

Click.

Click-click.

Click-click-click.

Lights flared to life in the metal ceiling above our heads, while illumination strips curved around the sides of the tunnel walls and ran along the floor, almost like arrows giving us directions. *Step this way.* There was more than enough light to see by, so I turned off my flashlight and hooked it to the bottom of my vest. Lulu did the same with her flashlight and Wynter's too.

We stood still and quiet, but all I could hear was the low, faint, steady hum of the lights. No voices, no screams, nothing else. I didn't know how far we might be from Frost's lab, but I wasn't going to risk the ubervillain taking us by surprise like he had Kyle and me in the park.

113

"Put your sunglasses on," I whispered, pulling my pair out of a pocket on my vest.

Lulu and Wynter both nodded and did as I asked. I dropped to my knees, fished out the pair of doggie goggles that I'd bought for Rascal at Oodles o' Stuff, and slipped them on over the puppy's head. Rascal wagged his tail, apparently liking his new gear.

I didn't know what the tunnel might have been used for, maybe some kind of maintenance or to move equipment from one side of the factory to the other, but it was more than wide enough for the three of us to walk side by side by side. After an initial sloped drop of about thirty feet, the tunnel leveled off and ran straight. The air was surprisingly fresh down here, smelling as crisp as it had aboveground. And it was just as cold too. I didn't know if that was because we were underground or approaching Frost's lair.

Every few feet, we would stop, look, and listen, but all I could see was more tunnel up ahead. We'd gone about a hundred feet into the corridor when another louder hum overpowered that of the lights. I listened, trying to figure out what it was, but it sounded like a really large refrigerator.

Wynter sighed.

"What's wrong?" I asked.

She shook her head. "Mysterious hums are never good, in my experience."

"Yeah," Lulu agreed. "Mysterious hums mean mysterious generators, which power mysterious machines, and villains never use those for anything nice."

I shivered, my worried thoughts chilling me more than the cold air did. But Kyle was wherever those machines were, so we walked on.

Eventually, we reached the end of the tunnel. A door was set into the metal wall in front of us, with a keypad off to one side.

Lulu studied the keypad, then shook her head. "I could rip

out the wires and probably bypass it, but I don't know how much time that might take or what sort of alarms that might set off."

"Kyle is running out of time," I said. "And Frost is bound to realize that we're here sooner or later, if he hasn't already. I say we use what Jasper gave us and blast right through it."

Wynter and Lulu nodded their agreement. Lulu took hold of Rascal's leash, and the three of them moved back out of the way.

I fished around in my vest pockets and pulled out one of the small, cherry-shaped bombs that Jasper had given me. I carefully fixed the bomb to where the door met the metal wall next to the keypad, pulled the stem out of the device, and scurried back up the tunnel to where Wynter, Lulu, and Rascal were standing.

Pop!

The bomb blast didn't seem any larger than that of a small firecracker, and the flames and smoke quickly died out, revealing a slightly dented and open door.

Wynter, Lulu, and I all held our breaths, wondering if the small explosion had been loud enough to attract Frost's attention. But the seconds passed, then turned into a minute...then two...then three...

No one came to investigate the noise, so Lulu passed Rascal's leash back over to me, and we approached the door. Wynter carefully eased it open wide enough for us to step through to the other side.

The door opened up into an enormous factory area filled with metal vats, loose pipes, and other dusty equipment that hadn't been used in years, except for a large generator in the corner that was lit up like a Christmas tree. Lulu was right in thinking that a generator was the source of that low, ominous hum we'd been hearing. But the good thing was that the hum was much louder here and more of a steady drone. It must have drowned out the noise of us blasting through the door, which meant we still had a chance to sneak up on Frost. More lights blazed up ahead. That was where his lab would be.

Wynter motioned at us, and we stopped and huddled together just inside the door.

"Let me go in first," she murmured. "Just like we planned. I'll keep Frost busy, if he's in there. You two focus on getting Swifte out of here and not dying yourselves. Okay?"

Lulu snapped her hand up in a cheeky salute. "Sir, yes, sir. I will do my very best not to die."

"Me too," I murmured.

Rascal barked his agreement not to die as well.

I just hoped that Kyle wasn't dead already. My heart dropped at the thought, but I forced my fear away. He was still alive, and he was going to stay that way. We *would* save him.

Wynter headed deeper into the factory. I made sure my sunglasses still covered my eyes, tightened my grip on Rascal's leash, and tiptoed after her. Lulu brought up the rear, moving much slower and putting her cane down with care so that it didn't *tap-tap-tap* against the metal floor. Despite the steady drone of the generator, Frost still had the supersenses he'd stolen from Radio Randall, and the slightest noise would alert him to our presence, something we needed to avoid if at all possible.

We reached a series of vats near the center of the area. Beyond the metal containers, the lights were much brighter and tinged with a cold, blue color—almost the same ice-blue as Frost's costume. Wynter hunkered down beside one of the vats. I dropped into a crouch beside her, and we both peered around the edge of the container, with Lulu and Rascal right behind us.

Frost's lab lay before us.

Vats circled the area like soldiers standing watch, before giving way to metal tables covered with pens, note pads, and plastic, ice-blue binders filled with reams of paper. Many of the tables looked like they'd come straight out of some high school chemistry lab, with burners embedded in the surface. Several of the burners were lit, the flames licking at the bottoms of glass beakers filled with all sorts of strange, bubbling, neon-colored liquids. The generator's hum wasn't nearly as loud here, but the air smelled of bleach and other harsh chemicals, and I had to pinch my nose to hold back a sneeze.

The evil, electrical heart of the lab was a row of laptops lining another table set off by itself, the precious equipment well away from all the bubbling liquid experiments. All sorts of ominous-looking tubes and wires snaked out of the computers, leading to a control panel bristling with knobs, buttons, levers, and blinking lights that had been welded onto the side of one of the vats.

A large metal ring had been placed over a hook jutting out from the control panel. It would have been nothing more than an oversize collar—if not for the dozens of needles attached to it. Needles that all pointed in and would jab deep into someone's neck when you snapped the collar around their throat.

Just like Frost had done to Blue.

I shuddered. It was exactly the sort of mad-scientist setup that you would expect, and one that I'd seen in photos in the library archives and dozens of times on SNN whenever the Fearless Five or the cops shut down an illegal ubervillain or drug lab.

But I looked past the tables, burners, and beakers to the most important thing in the lab—Swifte.

He was standing up against a metal slab, his outstretched arms and legs shackled to it, making him look like a human star. His white costume still covered his body, but he wasn't wearing his winged mask. Beside me, Wynter sucked in a breath at the revelation of Swifte's real identity as Kyle Quicke.

"I should have known," Wynter whispered, shaking her head. "Nobody can cook that much that fast for that many heroes and villains."

We huddled beside the vat, looking and listening, but I didn't see or hear anything out of the ordinary, not even Frost, puttering around somewhere. Kyle slumped against his shackles, as if he'd already used up all of his energy trying to break free of them and had realized how useless it was. The metal cuffs gleamed like they were made out of pure solidium. Even Wynter, with all her superstrength, would have had a hard time busting out of them.

Wynter touched my shoulder. "Stay here," she whispered. "I'm going to get Kyle out of those shackles. Maybe we can slip out of here before Frost comes back, get the Fearless Five to come surround the lab, and force Frost to give himself up."

"Be careful," I whispered back.

Wynter squeezed my shoulder and got to her feet. Lulu slid forward and took her place beside me, with Rascal huddled next to her.

Wynter tiptoed around the edges of the lab, moving from vat to vat, being as quiet as possible as she worked her way over to Kyle. I bit my lip to keep from calling out Kyle's name and letting him know that we were here, that I was here, and that we were going to rescue him.

Finally, Wynter got close enough to leave the vats behind, and she made a beeline to where Kyle was shackled in the center of the lab. He looked up at the soft sound of her footsteps on the metal floor. His blue eyes widened, then narrowed in thought. He glanced around, as if looking for Frost and making sure that the coast was clear.

Wynter hurried over to his side and studied the solidium cuffs that shackled him to the metal slab.

"If I rescue you, does this mean that I get free meals for life at Quicke's?" she quipped in a soft voice.

He grinned. "You better believe it. I'll even throw in free drinks. I know how much you love a good cosmopolitan."

"How generous of you," she quipped back, pushing her sunglasses up onto the top of her head.

"But how did you find me?" Kyle frowned. "And why are you wearing sunglasses this far underground?"

"Piper," Wynter said, leaning down and peering at his shackles. "She was the one who figured out where you were. The glasses were her idea. Now, let's get these cuffs off you and get out of here—"

"I'm afraid that's not going to happen," a loud voice cut in.

Frost suddenly appeared by the control panel, his freezoray gun clutched in his hand. I blinked. How had he done that? I hadn't heard or even seen him... Catwalk, I realized. He still had her ability to move without making a sound, along with Blue's speed. He must have heard us blast through the door after all and had used his stolen powers to hide in the shadows while Wynter approached Kyle.

"Wynter," Frost called out. "So nice of you to join my little party. I was just about to relieve Mr. Quicke of his speedy superpowers. I'll give you the honor of draining your superstrength out of you next, along with your ice abilities. I'm afraid to say that my own cold powers have been on the fritz ever since I was caught in that horrible explosion here. It'll be nice to have those back again."

Wynter's hands clenched into fists. "Bring it on."

Frost leveled his freezoray gun at her. "With pleasure."

He pulled the trigger, and a blast of cold shot out of the end of the barrel. Wynter threw herself down onto the floor, rolled out of the way, and popped right back up onto her feet. Blue flames flashed to life in her palms before morphing into two snowballs studded with long, sharp icicles. Wynter flung her hands out, sending the projectiles shooting out at Frost.

The spiked snowballs streaked through the air toward the ubervillain—

And Frost simply stepped out of the way. The snowballs *thunk-thunked* into the metal vat behind him, icicles shattering on impact, but Frost had already used his stolen speed to move all the way over to the other side of the lab, right behind Wynter.

Even as I opened my mouth to scream that he was behind her, Wynter turned around, as if sensing where Frost was.

But it was too late.

This time, instead of using his freezoray gun, Frost waved his hand, just like he had at me in Paradise Park. I knew what was coming next.

Sure enough, a second later, a burst of intense light filled the room, as though we were standing in the center of the sun.

Wynter had pushed her sunglasses up on top of her head to examine Kyle's shackles, and she'd forgotten to put them back down over her eyes. She screamed in pain as Frost used Catwalk's light power to sear her retinas. I was still wearing my sunglasses, and even with them, the light was almost blinding. Beside me, Lulu winced and hissed, while Rascal whimpered, despite the dark doggie goggles on his head.

Wynter fell to her knees, screaming and covering her eyes, even though the light had already faded away. Frost circled around and around her, like she was a bug that he was about to squash with the toe of his ice-blue forty-two boot. Then he used his speed to zip over to the control panel and yank down one of the levers on it.

Wynter must have been kneeling on some sort of trapdoor because the floor opened up beneath her, and she disappeared from sight. A second later, I heard the *thud* of her body hitting the bottom of a hole, along with a low groan. She was still alive, but for how long? There was no telling what sort of torture devices Frost might have stashed down in that hole.

Frost stood at the edge of the trapdoor, staring down into the space, but whatever he saw must have satisfied him because he went back over to the control panel and started fiddling with the buttons and switches there. Every once in a while, Wynter would let out another groan, but she was out of the fight for now.

Which meant that it was up to me to save her and Kyle.

Or die trying.

CHAPTER TWELVE

"Now what?" Lulu muttered. "Our ace in the hole just literally went down into a hole."

"Now you go back up the tunnel," I whispered. "Hopefully, the Fearless Five are done cleaning up that interstate accident by now. You have to get them over here as soon as possible. And take Rascal with you."

I passed the puppy's leash over to Lulu, who stared at me.

"And what are you going to do?"

I let out a breath. "At best, save Kyle and Sabrina from Frost."

"And at worst?"

I winced. I didn't want to think about it.

Lulu chewed her lip, obviously not wanting to leave me.

"Go," I whispered. "Somebody has to tell the Fearless Five what's going on. They know you, which means that you have a better chance of getting through to them in time than I do. Besides, I'm not leaving Kyle and Sabrina down here."

Lulu didn't like it, but she nodded. "Good luck," she whispered. "I'll be back with help as soon as I can."

I nodded back. Lulu got to her feet and headed out of the

factory, taking Rascal along with her. The puppy gave me a worried look, but he turned and went with Lulu. In a few seconds, they both disappeared from sight.

I patted down all the pockets and items hanging off my vest, doing a mental inventory and wondering how I could best use my supplies to save Kyle. Then I started unzipping the pockets, ripping open all those chemical packs I'd bought, and stuffing them back inside my vest.

Doubt filled me the whole time I worked. Cold, horrible, terrible doubt. Frost was one of the worst of the worst. He had his freezoray gun, a whole bunch of stolen superpowers, and who knew what else down here in his lab. Did I really think that I could go up against him and win? Me, Piper Perez, an ordinary woman with absolutely no superpowers whatsoever? Even my inner fandemic knew exactly how badly this was probably going to turn out.

But all my doubts and fears didn't matter. If I didn't do this, if I didn't at least *try*, Kyle was dead, and Sabrina along with him. I wasn't about to let Frost hurt them, much less drain them of their blood and powers. Not as long as I still had breath left to fight.

So I thought about Frost, his freezoray gun, and everything I knew about all the other people that he'd killed. Radio Randall. Musclular Mila. Catwalk. Bustling Blue. Their powers. Their strengths. And especially their weaknesses.

With all that information churning and churning in my mind, I let out a breath. Then I made sure my sunglasses were still on tight, got to my feet, and stepped out into the middle of the lab.

"Step away from the control panel," I ordered in the loudest, toughest voice I could.

"Piper!" Kyle yelled and started struggling against his shackles again. "What are you doing? Get out of here! Run! Now!"

"I'm here to save you," I said. "And I'm not going anywhere until I do."

Frost glanced over his shoulder. After a moment, he sighed. "You again. I would have thought that once would have been enough, but apparently, some people are agonizingly slow learners. You know, Ms. Perez, I was going to let you live, since you don't have any powers worth taking. No powers at all, as a matter of fact. But this will work out even better. It will be so much more fun to kill you first, then listen to Swifte scream when he realizes that he's the reason you're dead."

Frost waved his hand, just like he had with Wynter a few minutes before, and that intense burst of light filled the lab. After a few seconds, the light faded away, with me still in the same position as before. Frost frowned as he realized why I was still standing and not writhing on the floor and screaming in pain.

"Sunglasses?" he asked. "Really?"

I shrugged. "Maybe you should have read up some on Catwalk. Sunglasses block the worst effects of her light power. All the photographers would wear them whenever they had to shoot one of her fashion shows to keep their eyes from getting fried."

"Well, look at the big brain on you," Frost said. "Good thing I don't need anyone else's power to get rid of you. I have plenty of my own."

He whipped out his freezoray gun from the holster on his belt and blasted me with a cold ray, but I was ready for that too. I hit a button, and warm air blasted over me, thanks to the miniature heater I'd hooked to my vest and all those chemical packets that I'd ripped open and stuffed into the pockets earlier. The heater and the packets didn't quite nullify the bitter, brutal chill of Frost's freezoray gun, but enough heat was radiating off my body to keep the cold ray from freezing me in place like an icicle hanging off a roof.

Frost lowered his gun, his eyes bulging wide at the fact that I wasn't subzero by now. Then he looked down at his weapon, as if he thought something was wrong with it. I doubted that it ever occurred to him that a lowly mortal like me had simply found a way to outsmart him, the oh-so-brilliant scientist.

Ubervillains. Always so overconfident.

Frost shoved his freezoray gun back into his holster. "No matter. I don't need my gun to kill you either. I can always just tear you apart with my bare hands."

He pulled off one glove, then the other, throwing them both down onto the floor. He held up his hands, and long, black talons shot out of his fingertips like spikes. I remembered Blue's horrible wounds, how it had looked like some animal had clawed him, along with the other victims.

Not an animal—Frost.

My chest tightened, but I didn't let him see my fear. "And who did you steal that power from?" I sniped.

"No one," he muttered. "It was a consequence of one of my experiments the last time I was here at this factory. When a dozen or so radioactive, genetically altered creatures bite and scratch you enough times, then your body absorbs some of those creatures' mutations. Lucky me, I got their talons. I haven't much cared for this particular side effect up until now, but I think it will be rather fun to carve you up with my new nails. Just like I did to your friend Blue."

Kyle struggled and struggled against his shackles, harder than ever before. "Run, Piper! Run!"

Frost let out a low, evil laugh. "Oh, yes, Piper. Go ahead and *run*. It'll make the chase so much more *fun*."

He headed across the lab, moving closer and closer to me. Kyle kept screaming and screaming, telling me to forget about him, telling me to *run-run-run*, but I tuned him out. We'd already wasted too much time being apart, and I wasn't about to leave him now.

Still, as Frost neared me, I wondered if I had made the right decision—or if being an overeager, know-it-all fandemic was finally going to get me killed.

I backed up, thinking about all the powers that Frost had collected. I still had on my sunglasses, so he couldn't blind me, and I was warm enough to melt the polar ice caps, thanks to my heater and all those chemical packets. In fact, I was uncomfortably warm, with sweat beading on my temples, but I didn't dare turn off the heater or rip off the vest for fear that Frost would reach for his freezoray gun again.

Frost let out a loud battle cry and charged forward, his talon-tipped fingernails arcing out as though he wanted to swipe them across my face and give me the same horrid scars that he had.

Only one thing to do.

I waited for him to get into range.

Then I stepped up and punched him in the jaw.

I'd never punched anyone or anything before, except the bag in my kickboxing class, and it hurt like you wouldn't believe. Pain exploded across my knuckles and roared up into my elbow and shoulder. But apparently, Frost wasn't used to being punched either because my blow, weak as it was, caused him to stop and stagger back. He blinked a few times, as though I'd walloped him harder than either one of us had realized.

But he got over it quickly—far too quickly.

Frost growled and charged at me again. This time, he used Blue's speed, and I barely managed to lunge out of the way of his vicious strike. Frost's fingers slammed into the vat behind where I had been standing a moment before. He growled again and ripped his talons through the metal like it was paper.

I winced at the terrible *screech-screech-screech*. I didn't know what kind of mutated animals might have bitten and scratched him, but I couldn't let Frost sink his talons into me. He would rip me apart with them, just like he'd promised.

Kyle realized that I wasn't going to leave him behind, and he kept yelling, this time shouting encouragements to me. "Get him! Kick his ass! Go, Piper! Go!"

Even though I was fighting for my life against an evil

ubervillain, a big, happy, goofy grin stretched across my face. For the first time in a long time, Kyle and I were on the same side, and it was a terrific feeling. In that moment, I felt strong, powerful, invincible, like I could do absolutely *anything*, even take on Frost and win.

So Frost and I went around and around the lab, with him trying to tear me into bloody pieces with his talons, and me avoiding him and landing what punches I could.

I ducked, and Frost rammed his talons into another vat, but this time, his hand got stuck. He cursed, trying to pull free. I used the opportunity to race over to the control panel, looking at all the buttons, levers, and switches, and trying to figure out which one would open Kyle's cuffs.

Screech-screech-screech.

Frost was tearing through the metal, which meant that I was almost out of time. So I just started hitting random buttons.

Every button I punched and every switch I threw definitely made stuff happen—all the wrong stuff.

The burners flared brighter and hotter, causing the neon-colored liquids in the beakers to bubble up. Some of the glass containers shattered outright under the intense heat, splattering fluid everywhere. Lights dimmed and brightened, and another trapdoor caved in right below Kyle's feet. But nothing opened his shackles.

"You clueless idiot!" Frost yelled. "Stop hitting buttons! You're wrecking my lab!"

I glanced over my shoulder to find him charging at me again. I managed to hit a few more buttons before I lunged out of the way of his latest strike. Frost stopped just short of slamming his talons into his own control panel. Too bad.

Wynter was still stuck in that pit in the floor, but by this point, she'd shaken off the effects of Frost's blinding light and the hard fall. Her *snowballs-snowballs-snowballs!* curses drifted up to me. From the sound of things, the walls of the pit were too slick for her to climb up, which meant I still had to find some way to stop Frost for good—

Frost came at me again, but I darted behind one of the metal tables, out of reach of his swiping talons. He still had Blue's speed, and it was just a matter of time before he managed to catch me with it. I needed to find a way to beat him—right now—or I was dead.

"Stand still!" Frost snarled.

"Dream on!" I yelled back.

Around and around the lab we went, both of us knocking over tables, beakers, binders, and more. Paper fluttered through the air like snow, while liquids splashed all over the floor, bubbling, burning, and oozing everywhere. I made sure to stay out of the bright, glowing pools. As much as I longed for a superpower, I didn't want to get turned into a monster either, which seemed to be what Frost specialized in.

I ducked his latest blow and ended up slamming my entire body up against one of the metal vats. Something dug into my stomach, and I realized that there was one trick I hadn't used yet.

The bullhorn.

Frost came at me again, but I ducked out of the way and ran to the other side of the lab. I whipped around, but he was still several feet behind me. My fingers dropped to the bullhorn, and I struggled to unhook it from the mesh of my vest.

I had just managed to free it when Frost charged at me again. I ducked, the way I had so many times before, but my boot slipped in one of the smoking puddles of ice-blue goo on the floor.

"Piper!" Kyle screamed, but there was nothing he could do to help me.

My arms windmilled, and my feet flew out from under me. I slammed into the control panel, hard enough to punch several more buttons there and make the lights flicker again. I bounced off, and my ass hit the floor a second later. The sharp blow dazed me, and I blinked and blinked, trying to get the world to stop spinning around and around like a crazy carnival ride.

I looked up to find Frost advancing on me, his eyes glowing a cold, sinister blue behind his jagged, icicle-shaped mask. I tried to curl my fingers into a fist to fight him off, but my hand was already wrapped around something hard and plastic. I glanced down and realized that I had managed to hang on to the bullhorn. New hope surged through me. This wasn't over yet.

"Piper! Piper!" Kyle kept screaming. "Leave her alone!"

Frost looked over at him and sneered. "I will—just as soon as I kill her."

Kyle's face paled with fear, and he strained and strained against his shackles, but he couldn't free himself. Kyle screamed again with rage, his muscles standing out in his neck, arms, chest, and legs, but he just wasn't strong enough to break those solidium cuffs.

Frost laughed and pulled his freezoray gun out of the holster on his belt, ready to finish me off with it at close range.

Kyle fixed his agonized gaze on me. "Piper," he whispered. "I'm so sorry for everything. I love you so much—"

His voice choked off, but I smiled back at him.

"I love you too," I said. "And don't you forget it."

"Oh, enough with the mushy stuff," Frost sneered. "You've been more than enough trouble already, Ms. Perez. Time for you to die!"

He snapped up his freezoray gun, and I lifted the bullhorn, pointing it straight at him. Instead of being concerned, Frost planted a hand on his thin hip and chuckled.

"And what do you think you're going to do with *that*?" he sneered.

I grinned. "This."

I pulled the trigger on the bullhorn, blasting static directly at the ubervillain. The sharp sound shrieked through the entire lab. Most folks say that nails on a chalkboard is the most horrible sound they've ever heard, but I've always thought that static was much, much worse. Or maybe that was because I'd spent so many nights wincing at the staticky feedback of the amps and speakers at The Blues, the karaoke bar that Abby and I frequented. And, more specifically, watching Abby grimace in pain as the screechy sound assaulted her supersenses and gave her an instant migraine.

Just like it was doing to Frost right now.

He had supersenses too, thanks to the powers he'd stolen from Radio Randall, and the static seemed to bother him even more than it did Abby. Maybe he hadn't had his abilities long enough to be able to fully control them yet. Frost screamed, dropped his freezoray gun, clapped his hands over his ears, and doubled over in front of me. But he didn't go down, so I cranked up the volume on the bullhorn another notch, then another one, until it was making even my ears hurt, despite the earplugs that Lulu had given me to block out the noise.

The bullhorn's static pushed Frost over the edge. The villain's head snapped up, and he suddenly seemed more animal than human, his face twisting and twisting, the jagged red scars there standing out in sharp relief against his pale skin. Spittle flew out of his lips as he screamed and screamed at me, even though the bullhorn drowned out all his many curses. But instead of coming at me again, he turned and ran, desperately trying to get away from the screeching static.

But he didn't remember the trapdoor he'd left open in the floor, and he ran right over it. For a moment, Frost's skinny legs seemed to churn in mid-air, like a cartoon character's would. Then he dropped down into the dark hole.

Thud.

Maybe it was just my imagination, but I could have sworn that I actually heard his body hit the bottom of the pit despite the staticky blare of the bullhorn. I turned off the device and tried to shake off the horrible ringing in my own ears.

I didn't know what was happening down in the hole, but all that mattered right now was freeing Kyle, so I got back up onto my feet and hit every single button on the control panel. I finally found the right one, and the cuffs on his wrists and ankles *clanked* open.

He staggered off the slab, sidestepping the second open trapdoor in the floor, and I was there to catch and steady him.

"Easy," I said. "Just take it easy for a minute."

Kyle stared at me. "You saved me, Piper."

I grinned. "What kind of Fandemic would I be if I let the love of my life die at the hands of an evil ubervillain? That wouldn't make for a very happy ending, now would it?"

Kyle chuckled, reached up, and gently pushed my sunglasses on top of my head. Then he cupped my cheek in his hand. "I said it before, and I'll say it again. I'm sorry that I've been such an idiot—about everything."

I leaned into his touch just like I had in the park, just like I always did, just like I always would. "Me too. But I love you, and you love me, and that's all that matters now. Right?"

"Right." Kyle leaned closer to me, his voice dropping to a low, husky whisper. "And going back to your apartment, like we'd planned earlier."

"Absolutely." I stood on my tiptoes, ready to kiss him—

"You! You get away from me!" a panicked voice rose up out of the pit.

Kyle and I broke apart and rushed over to the edge of the hole. Fifteen feet below, Frost was lying on the floor, his body sprawled at an awkward angle.

"Hello, Frost," Wynter purred, looming over him and cracking her knuckles. "Long time, no see. Let me reintroduce you to my fists."

Punch-punch-punch-punch.

Within seconds, Frost was curled into a ball on the floor, screaming that he surrendered already. Wynter hit him one more time for good measure, knocking him out cold, then peered up at me.

"Nice job, Piper," she said. "You can be my sidekick any time."

"Sidekick?" Kyle called out. "Forget that. She's a superhero, and she's all mine."

He pulled me close. I grinned, wrapped my arms around his neck, and kissed him.

CHAPTER THIRTEEN

Among the debris in the lab, I found a long piece of rope that I threw down to Wynter so she could climb up out of the pit. Wynter hauled Frost up as well and shackled him to his own metal slab. The villain was still unconscious, but we weren't taking any chances.

By the time we got Frost locked away and left the lab, Lulu had reached the Fearless Five, and the superheroes had arrived at the factory ruins. Well, really, it was just four of them, since Chief Newman was here as himself, along with several cops.

I explained to the chief and Fiera how Frost had kidnapped Swifte, how I'd tracked them down, and how I'd managed to defeat the ubervillain.

"Well done, Piper," the chief rumbled. "Very well done. Don't worry about Frost anymore. My men and I will take care of him."

He gestured to some of his officers, and they walked down the ramp into the lab to retrieve the ubervillain.

"You beat Frost with a bullhorn?" Fiera said, looking at me with new respect. "That's impressive."

I shrugged. "I know someone with supersenses. It wasn't too hard to figure out."

Fiera sniffed, threw her blond hair over her shoulder, and strode over to talk to Hermit, Karma Girl, and Striker, who were standing with Wynter, Lulu, and Rascal.

"Supersenses?" Kyle whispered, having put his mask back on and resumed his Swifte persona. "Who has supersenses?"

"Abby," I whispered back.

"Ah," he said, his face clearing. "So that's why she's so cranky all the time."

I laughed. "I wouldn't say that, but she definitely doesn't like loud noises. And neither did Frost."

The two of us watched while the cops marched Frost out of the lab and over to a waiting police van. The cops had put solidium cuffs on the ubervillain's wrists and ankles to keep him from escaping, and he could only manage a slow, steady shuffle. Frost alternated between glaring at me, Swifte, and Wynter, his blue eyes bright with anger.

I shivered and turned away from him. I'd made a dangerous enemy today, but the police would lock Frost away in some supermax ubervillain prison where he would never see the light of day again. That was my hope, anyway. Even if I knew that Fiona was right. Ubervillains never seemed to stay dead—or imprisoned—for very long.

Once Frost was secured in the back of the police van, Chief Newman came over to question Kyle, er, Swifte.

I drifted away, standing off by myself. Eventually, Fiera came over to me, with Karma Girl trailing along behind her. Fiera stood by my side in silence for several seconds.

"*So*," she drawled out the word. "You called my phone earlier, trying to get me to come help Swifte."

"So?"

She cleared her throat. "So…you called Fiona's phone."

With everything that had been going on, I'd forgotten all about that. "Yeah. I did, didn't I?"

Fiera, Fiona, stared at me. "How long have you known?"

I shrugged. "For a while now."

"How did you find out?" she asked.

"I heard you talking on your phone to your father one day. The way you were chatting about heroes and villains…it was sort of obvious that you were one."

Fiera slapped her hands on her hips, red-hot sparks shooting out of her fingertips. "You eavesdropped on me!"

"I did no such thing," I shot right back. "I was sitting in my office working, just like always. Even with the door shut, I could still hear you. If you don't want people to find out about your supersecret identity, then you shouldn't talk so loud on your phone. Or so often. I can't even tell you how many times I've heard you discussing Fearless Five business with Chief Newman or Sam Sloane. And you definitely shouldn't eat so much food where other people can see you all the time."

Fiera sniffed, crossed her arms over her chest, and tossed her blond hair back over her shoulder. Karma Girl chuckled.

"Come on, Fiera," Karma Girl said. "That last one is kind of a dead giveaway."

Fiera glared at her teammate. "Well, if Piper knows who I am, then she knows who we all are, including you, *Carmen Cole*."

Karma Girl shrugged. "It was only a matter of time before someone figured out who I really was." She grinned. "You might even say that it was *karmic retribution* for me exposing the identities of all those other heroes and villains."

Fiera groaned at her cheesy joke, then turned her gaze back to me. "Well, if you know I'm a superhero and why I eat so much all the time, then why do you keep putting all those eating disorder pamphlets on my desk?"

"Because all the sales clerks and workers wonder how you can eat so much and stay so thin," I replied. "One of them made a remark about you secretly being a superhero. Since I didn't want you to blow your own secret identity, I told everyone that you had an eating disorder and made sure that all the workers knew about those pamphlets I put on your desk. I know it was a terrible thing to do, but I was just trying to help."

Fiera's face softened. "You're a good friend, Piper."

I grinned. "Yeah. I know."

I bumped her shoulder with my own. Fiera laughed and bumped me back, almost sending me spinning down to the ground with her incredible strength.

Fiera and Karma Girl went over to wrap up things with Hermit, Striker, Chief Newman, and the rest of the cops.

Swifte, Wynter, and Lulu walked over to me, with the computer hacker leading Rascal on his leash. I dropped to my knees and rubbed Rascal's ears, just the way he liked. Which, of course, caused the puppy to flop down onto his back for a tummy rub, which Swifte took care of.

Lulu handed over Rascal's leash to me. "Well, Piper, I'll say this for you and Abby. You girls certainly know how to party."

I laughed. "Yeah, I guess we do. We should get lunch sometime. You, me, Abby." I looked at Wynter. "And you too."

She cracked her knuckles. "Only if there are more ubervillains to pummel."

"I don't know about that, but I'm sure I could buy you a round of Wynter cosmopolitans at Quicke's."

Wynter winked at me. "It's a date."

I laughed again, then hugged her and Lulu, knowing that I'd made two new friends.

The cops and the Fearless Five were still processing the scene, especially everything in Frost's underground lab, but there was nothing else for us to do here. So Lulu fired up her van, and Wynter, Swifte, Rascal, and I piled inside for the ride back into the city.

Thirty minutes later, Lulu pulled up outside of my building, and Swifte, Rascal, and I got out of her van.

"You kids have fun with your crazy makeup sex," Lulu called out through the window before she and Wynter zoomed away.

I grinned and waved back at them.

Swifte, Rascal, and I went up to my apartment. The puppy bounded inside, sniffing everything the way he always did, but I suddenly felt awkward and unsure. Heartfelt confessions of love were all well and good when our lives were in danger, but now that we were safe, I wasn't quite sure how to start over. And Kyle didn't seem any more certain than I did, judging by the way he kept running the toe of his white sneaker across the floor instead of looking at me.

"I need to make some calls," he said, finally breaking the silence. "Check in with Ray, and see how he's handling everything at the restaurant."

"Of course."

He went back into my bedroom to use the phone there. I puttered around for several minutes, making sure that Rascal had plenty of food and water for the night. But finally, there was nothing else to do but stare at my closed bedroom door and listen to the murmur of Kyle's voice.

Come on, Piper! Snap out of it! This was Kyle. The guy I'd dated for a year. The guy that I'd just battled an ubervillain for. The love of my life. There was no reason to be uncertain or unsure. Not anymore. Never again. We'd already wasted too much time being apart, and I wasn't about to lose another second with him.

So I lifted my chin, squared my shoulders, and marched over to my bedroom door, quickly opening, then closing it behind me.

Kyle was waiting for me.

He had already finished his call and stood at the foot of my bed. Once again, we faced each other, the silence stretching out between us. But the longer I stared at Kyle, the more emotions flashed in his eyes. Need. Desire. Care. Concern. Love.

So much love. And I knew that the feeling was reflected in my own gaze.

I stepped forward and wet my lips, ready to tell him how much I loved him—

WHOOSH!

One second, I was standing in front of Kyle. The next, we were on the bed, lying side by side, kissing furiously. All our earlier awkwardness and hesitation melted in an instant, and all I could think about was kissing him deeper and pulling him closer.

So I did.

I traced my hands over Kyle's shoulders, then trailed my fingers down his chest, searching for a zipper or string or something that would let me get past his spandex suit and touch all of his warm, delicious skin.

"How does this stupid thing even open?" I grumbled.

"You're in the *Slaves for Superhero Sex* club, and you don't know how to get into a superhero suit?" he teased. "Your fellow club members would be so disappointed in you, Piper."

I glared at him.

He laughed. "Here. Let me."

WHOOSH!

A second later, Kyle was lying next to me, naked.

WHOOSH!

The second after that, he'd gotten rid of my clothes as well.

"Much better." I grinned. "You know, I think this is the best use of your speed power I've seen so far."

Kyle grinned back at me. "Oh, baby. You haven't seen anything yet."

I drew him down on top of me, kissing him even harder than before, even as my hands roamed over his body, caressing his lean muscles. I breathed in, drinking in his unique scent. I'd always thought Kyle smelled crisp and clean, like a literal breath of fresh air, and now I knew why.

Being with him was so familiar and yet so different at the

same time. Because now I knew about every part of him, alter ego and all.

We already knew what the other liked. Where to kiss. Where to lick. Where to caress. And we both set out to bring as much pleasure to the other as possible.

Kyle nibbled on my neck while I ran my fingers through his hair. His hands cupped my breasts, squeezing gently, while I stroked my fingers over him. Then it was his turn to stroke me while I kissed his chest.

Finally, Kyle covered himself with a condom, and I opened my arms, drawing him down on top of me. I took birth control pills, but we still used extra protection. I groaned as Kyle slid into me, filling me the way he had so many times in the past. And just like before when we were together, he moved inside me, then withdrew one inch at a time before surging forward again in a long, slow, deliberate stroke.

I pulled him even closer, eager to fall into the rhythm that we both knew so well, but Kyle gently held me still.

"Now, Piper, you know I like to take my time with these sorts of things," he teased, nipping the sensitive skin of my neck with his teeth again.

"Really? You sure you want to keep playing your waiting game?" I shifted my hips forward, taking him even deeper inside me. "Because I can think of a much more interesting game to play."

He groaned in response, and our lips crashed together in a hot, hard kiss. Kyle began to move inside me in earnest, and I met him kiss for kiss, stroke for stroke, thrust for thrust until we both found our release.

Together.

Again. Finally. At last.

Afterward, we lay cuddled under the fleece sheets together. My head was pillowed on Kyle's shoulder, and I was tracing random patterns on his chest.

"I've missed this," he said in a soft voice. "I've missed you so much, Piper. I've been such an idiot."

"I think we both have."

He gave me a lopsided grin. "You mean wasting these last few months by looking longingly at each other, instead of actually being together?"

"Among other things." I scooted up so that my face was next to his on the pillows. "I want you to know that I went to the factory tonight to rescue you, Kyle Quicke, the man I love. Not Swifte, not a superhero. You—just *you*."

"Yeah, I think that's finally sinking in through my thick skull. Sorry it took me so long." He paused. "Usually I'm much…swifter than that."

I groaned. "And now you're making bad superhero puns about your own power and persona."

His grin widened. "Well, you do know my secret identity. If I can't make bad jokes about it with you, then who can I make them with?"

I looped my arms around his neck. "I love your bad jokes, just like I love the rest of you Kyle 'Swifte' Quicke. And I always will."

"And that's something that I'll never, ever get tired of hearing," he whispered before lowering his lips to mine again.

EPILOGUE

One month later

"And now, I am pleased to announce the winner of the award for the most outstanding project volunteer...Piper Perez!"

A voice boomed through the sound system, and a spotlight fell on me. I smiled into the glare, not minding at all that it seared my eyes almost as badly as Frost's stolen power had all those weeks ago. I lifted my hand and waved, and the crowd erupted into cheers.

After a few seconds, the spotlight dimmed enough for me to see what I was doing. Kyle was sitting next to me, clapping almost as fast as he could run. Abby and Wesley were sitting with us, and they were all cheering for me.

Kyle leaned over and kissed my cheek, before pulling my chair out and helping me to my feet. I walked up onto the stage that had been erected in front of the bar to receive my award from the library director. She shook my hand, and we grinned into another spotlight, posing for photos. Then I left the stage and went back to my seat.

Earlier tonight had been the grand opening of *A Bigtime Past*, a chance for the public to wander through the library exhibit and see all the photos, memorabilia, and more that the volunteers, including me, had collected for the history project. The opening had been a smashing success, with scores of folks crowding into the library, along with reporters and city officials. Now, we were all at Quicke's for a reception, enjoying drinks and desserts as the library officials recognized various folks for their help with and contributions to the project. I'd been thrilled when they'd told me that I was getting an award, and it had been the perfect end to a perfect evening.

I left the stage, stopping to shake hands and accept congrats from folks. All of my friends were here tonight, including Lulu, Sabrina, Fiona, and Chief Newman, although everyone was dressed as their real selves instead of as their superhero alter egos.

Kelly Caleb was also here, doing a live stand-up news spot for SNN. She'd already interviewed me, and I couldn't wait to watch the news later on tonight. I'd also given Carmen Cole plenty of quotes for the story she was writing about the library project for *The Exposé* newspaper.

I finally made it back to my table and put down my award, which was shaped like a pink crystal heart. Then I looked up at the Bustling Blue lunch box that was sitting on a shelf on the brick wall. I'd restored the box, and Kyle had put it in a place of honor in the restaurant. Sadness flickered through me that Blue wasn't here to see it or the library project, but I knew that he would have gotten a kick out of all this, especially knowing that he was now enshrined at Quicke's with the rest of Bigtime's heroes and villains.

"I'm so proud of you!" Abby said, coming over to hug me.

"Me too," Wesley chimed in.

"Thanks, guys." I frowned and looked around. "But where did Kyle go—"

"Right here."

I blinked, and suddenly, Kyle was standing by my side, handing out glasses of champagne to our friends.

Abby raised her glass high. "To Piper!" she said in a loud, proud voice.

"To Piper!" Kyle and Wesley chimed in.

We all *clinked* our glasses together and sipped our champagne, and I could feel exactly how wide and goofy my smile was. This was one of the best nights of my life, and I didn't know what could possibly make it any better.

Abby set her glass down on the table, pulled her phone out of a pocket on her black fisherman's vest, and checked the time.

"And now, someone has to go pose for more photos," Abby said, snatching my glass out of my hand and putting it down onto the table next to hers. "Let's go, Piper. We have a strict schedule to keep."

Abby had planned this party the way she did so many others, which was one of the reasons why everything was so fabulous. Except for her nagging me about being where I was supposed to be at the right time. But everything else was so perfect that I didn't mind.

I laughed and held my hands up in mock surrender. "Okay, okay. Point me to the cameras."

Abby marched me over to where the library director was posing for photos, along with the other volunteers who'd been involved with the project. I thought she would stand there and oversee the photo shoot, but she hurried back over to Kyle and started talking to him. I wondered what they were up to, but the cameras flashed, and I was too busy smiling to worry about anything else.

I posed for several more photos, then spent the next two hours mixing and mingling with all the other guests, including many folks who were members of the *Slaves for Superhero Sex* club and had dressed up as their favorite heroes and villains to help celebrate the library project.

For once, I felt like I had Kyle's superspeed because the evening seemed to pass by in the blink of an eye. One minute, I was getting my award. The next, all the guests were drifting toward the doors, and the party was winding down.

I plopped down in my chair and let out a tired breath. I loved parties, but they were still a little overwhelming. I didn't know how Abby could plan and attend so many of them without being totally exhausted all the time.

Abby was one of the few folks who was still here, overseeing the restaurant workers as they cleaned up. But even that was going quickly, and Abby shooed Ray, the last of the waiters, into the back of the restaurant, stopped by the double doors, and looked over at me.

"Enjoy the rest of your night," she called out, grinning almost as big as I had been earlier.

I wondered what she was so happy about, but I waved at her, and she stepped into the back of the restaurant.

Soft footsteps sounded behind me, and Kyle appeared and took the chair next to mine. He nodded at my crystal award, which was still sitting on the table.

"How does it feel?" he asked. "Being the volunteer of volunteers?"

I laughed. "Pretty good. I'm so honored that the library chose me." My gaze drifted back over to the lunch box sitting on the shelf. "I just wish Blue had been here to see it."

Kyle reached over and squeezed my hand. "I'm sure he was here in spirit. And that he'll always be here in spirit now."

I squeezed back. "Thank you for that and the lunch box and everything else."

"Don't thank me just yet. The grand finale is still to come." Kyle held up his finger. "Sit still. I'll be back in a second."

WHOOSH!

And he literally was back in a second, presenting me with a white plate that featured a delicious-looking chocolate cake with a Swifte action figure perched on top. Something sparkled on the cake, and I leaned forward to get a better look at it.

A beautiful diamond ring was nestled in Swifte's open, outstretched palm.

My breath caught in my throat. "Kyle…"

I'd thought that nothing could make this night better, but this was…this was…*perfect.*

Kyle and I had been spending a lot of time together these past few weeks, getting to know each other in a deeper, more meaningful way than ever before, now that I knew his secret identity as Swifte. Our relationship wasn't perfect, but now that all our secrets were out in the open, we were back together and stronger than ever before.

And I had finally realized that being a superhero wasn't as glamorous as I'd always thought it would be. Sure, Kyle's power was supercool, but getting out of bed at three in the morning to go save someone who was in trouble could get a little tiresome after a while, even for the most dedicated and noblest of heroes. Not to mention all the money he spent on masks and costumes. And how hard it was to find opalescent white spandex. Even Oodles o' Stuff had a very limited supply of it, something that I needed to ask Sabrina to fix.

Don't get me wrong. I still wouldn't mind having a superpower (or two…or three… I wasn't picky, remember?), but I didn't go out of my way to seek one out anymore either. No more picking up scary-looking bugs. No more getting close to exotic zoo animals. I even canceled my reservation for my annual tour of the Bigtime Nuclear Power Plant.

And I wasn't one of the people that Kyle and the other heroes saved. Not anymore. Ever since the fight at the ice cream factory, I hadn't been in harm's way a single time. No runaway buses, no fires, no trouble of any sort had found me. Maybe it was karma. Maybe the universe was finally giving me a break. Maybe the powers that be had realized that facing down Frost had been enough danger to last me for the rest of my life. That's what I hoped, anyway, even if I had a funny feeling that it wouldn't last long.

But that was okay too. Because I'd proven that I could take care of myself, with or without superpowers, and I was stronger than ever before. And I was so proud of that—that I could be just as strong as any hero in my own special Fandemic way.

"I thought this would be the perfect end to the perfect night," Kyle said in a soft voice.

He plucked the ring out of the hand of his plastic alter ego, then got down on one knee beside me. "Piper Perez," he said, his voice husky with emotion. "Would you do me the biggest honor of all and be my wife—"

For once, I was quicker than he was because I threw myself into his arms before he'd finished asking me the question. "Yes, yes, yes!" I said, laughing and crying and smiling all at the same time.

Kyle grinned. "I was hoping you would say that."

He slipped the ring onto my finger. It fit perfectly. Just like the two of us did.

I held up the ring, admiring it for a moment before leaning forward, cupping his face in my hands, and capturing his lips with mine, melting into the moment, melting into the kiss, melting into him the way I always did—

"It's about time," a voice called out. "You were supposed to have proposed three minutes and thirteen seconds ago."

Kyle and I broke apart to find Abby standing by one of the open double doors, staring at us, with Rascal at her feet. The puppy barked, wanting to get in on the action after staying in the kitchen during the party, but Kyle made a shooing motion with his hand. Abby grinned before retreating back into the kitchen with Rascal and leaving us alone again.

Kyle grabbed my hands and pulled me to my feet. "What do you say we get out of here and go somewhere a little more private to continue our celebration?" he murmured.

"That sounds like the best idea I've heard all night," I murmured back. "Now kiss me again, Mr. Quicke."

"My pleasure, Ms. Perez," he whispered, his blue eyes shimmering with all the emotions I was feeling right now.

Love. Hope. Happiness. All so big and bright and beautiful that I thought my heart would burst from all the joy I was feeling in this moment.

Kyle grinned and lowered his lips to mine for a slow, lingering kiss. Taking his time and doing it the right way, just like I knew he would when we were alone.

Together.

Always.

Now and forever.

NIGHTINGALE

A BIGTIME NOVEL

NEW YORK TIMES
BESTSELLING AUTHOR

JENNIFER
ESTEP

NIGHTINGALE

by

JENNIFER ESTEP

BOOK FOUR IN THE BIGTIME SERIES

Anxious brides. Drunken businessmen. Panicked partygoers. As Bigtime, New York's premiere event planner, Abby Appleby is capable of handling almost any crisis, but even she's not prepared when she finds herself in the middle of a fight between superhero Talon and his ubervillain nemesis Bandit. Abby manages to save Talon, but the superhero is temporarily blinded, so she takes him back to her loft, where the two wait out a snowstorm. During a blizzard that shuts down the city, Abby and Talon grow close, and he starts calling her Nightingale because of her love of music and singing.

But Abby is afraid of what Talon will think when he can see the real her, so she conceals her identity from the sexy superhero, and they go their separate ways. However, Abby discovers that Talon is looking for Nightingale, looking for her—and so is Bandit. The mercenary ubervillain thinks that Abby has information that belongs to his boss, the mysterious Tycoon. Abby knows that she's in serious trouble and that not even Talon—or the Fearless Five—may be able to save her....

CHAPTER ONE

Sometimes, I really hate parties.

Especially engagement parties.

I hate the nose-watering flowers. The overpriced food. The endless champagne toasts. The hours-long parade of pomp, circumstance, and well wishes. The mushy exchanges of *I love you* that fail to last through the night, when the bride-to-be catches her fiancé in the broom closet with her best friend.

Most of all, I hate the unending crises surrounding any party—especially those of the rich and socially elite in Bigtime, New York.

Too bad I make my living planning such events.

A ragged breath cut through my dark reverie. I stood in a small antechamber deep inside the Bigtime Convention Center and Orchestra Hall. A woman dressed in a sequined, scarlet gown slouched in a chair in front of me, her head almost to her knees.

"This…is…wrong…Abby," Olivia O'Hara wheezed. "This…is a…mistake. We're doing this…for…all…the wrong…reasons."

Another night, another debutante, another cosmic meltdown ten minutes before the party started. This scenario had played itself out so many times before I could have calculated it down to the second, although most folks waited until their actual wedding day before panicking. Debutantes. They were even more temperamental than the superheroes and ubervillains who populated the sprawling city of Bigtime.

"It's not a terrible mistake." I raised my green eyes heavenward, asking for patience. I'd given this pep talk more than once too. "You care about Paul, don't you?"

Olivia hesitated. Her eyes dropped to the teardrop-shaped diamond on her left hand. She nodded again, stronger this time.

"As long as you care about him, it's not a *terrible* mistake. And if it is, well, that's what divorce lawyers are for. Just ask Joanne James. I'm sure she knows some good ones. Now, breathe into the bag before you start hyperventilating again."

She stuck her nose and mouth back into the brown paper bag I'd given her two minutes earlier. Olivia might be having a nervous breakdown, but she took care not to smear her perfect makeup. That alone told me she was going to walk into the party right on schedule.

Of course, Olivia O'Hara wouldn't smear her makeup anyway. Her family owned Oomph, one of the biggest makeup companies in the city. She'd been born with a mascara wand in one hand and lip liner in the other.

Still, if Olivia wasn't being so careful of her face, or worse, started pulling the diamond-studded clips from her hair, well, then I'd be worried.

Soft jazz music drifted in from the main auditorium. I checked my watch and nodded in approval. The band started right on time. Olivia couldn't hear the music. Nobody could have from this distance, unless they had superhearing—like me.

Don't get me wrong. I'm not a superhero. Not like the Fearless Five, Debonair, Swifte, or any of the other dozens of heroes who call Bigtime home. I don't dress up in formfitting spandex. Don't wear a mask. Don't call myself by another name.

And I *definitely* don't go around fighting crime. I have enough trouble handling the crises at my events.

A couple of years ago, though, I just happened to have acquired supersenses, thanks to a spilled amaretto sour and an over-electrified amp at a karaoke bar. Enhanced eyesight. Supersharp hearing. A heightened sense of touch. Souped-up taste buds. A nose that can smell cheeseburgers a mile away. I got the whole shebang, thanks to a couple thousand volts of electricity surging through my body.

Olivia kept wheezing, shooting looks at the closed door in front of us. I checked my watch again. Seven minutes and thirteen seconds until Olivia was supposed to make her grand entrance with Paul. Time to bring out the big guns.

I unzipped a pocket on the vest covering my upper body. The khaki mesh didn't quite go with the black pants, silk camisole, and jacket I wore, but I didn't care. My vest was better than the fanciest gown because the multiple pockets, zippers, and hidey holes contained my supplies. Today, I'd stocked it with my party gear. Bobby pins, glue, extra panty hose, clear nail polish, bandages, antacid, smelling salts, and a little pharmaceutical help—all of which were perfect for dealing with anxious, drunken, and unruly partygoers.

"Here." I shoved my brown hair off my shoulder and pulled a white pill out of one of the upper pockets. "Take this."

"What is it?" Olivia asked, staring at the tablet with suspicion.

"Something to help you relax. You want to relax, don't you? After all, this is your big night—the only engagement party you're ever going to have."

Probably.

"If you say so, Abby."

I checked my watch. Six minutes, thirty seconds. "I say so. Now take the pill."

I pulled out a small bottle of water from the side of my vest and handed it to her. Olivia swallowed the pill, washing it down with the water. Really, the pill wasn't all that potent, only having the effect of one good, stiff drink, but just the act of taking it helped most people, including Olivia. Her tight face relaxed, and her brown eyes softened. The nervous edge melted away. She'd be all right now.

I gave it another thirty seconds just to be on the safe side, then moved toward the door. "Are you ready? Paul is waiting for you."

Olivia stood, smoothing the wrinkles out of her dress. "I'm ready."

I opened the door.

Octavia O'Hara, Olivia's sister, paced outside, while Olivia's fiancé, Paul Potter, slouched in a chair. With black hair, deep brown eyes, and crimson lips, Octavia was a slightly older, sultrier version of her sister. Paul wore square glasses, and his pale, thinning, blond hair flopped over his forehead, no matter how many times he pushed it off his face.

"Is she okay?" Octavia asked. "Has she finally decided to come out? Or do I need to remind her how much money we've spent on this?"

I nodded. "Olivia's fine now. She just needed someone to calm her down. You know how jittery brides-to-be can be."

Well, she probably didn't. Octavia ran Oomph and was one of the most respected businesswomen in the city. I'd never seen her get jittery, nervous, or upset about anything, even when her father, Otto, died last year in a boating accident on Bigtime Bay. I'd planned his funeral, and Octavia had been the proverbial rock. I hadn't even seen her cry—not once. Olivia, on the other hand, had been a hysterical, weeping basket case.

Octavia nodded. "Thank you, Abby. I'm glad you were able

to get the door open and we didn't have to resort to more extreme measures."

I gave her a modest smile. "That's what I'm here for. To see to these little crises."

Olivia had only locked the door. All I had to do was dig through my vest pockets until I found the master key to the convention center, which I kept handy for just such emergencies. If Olivia had done something more difficult, like move a dresser in front of the door, I would have had to get some of the custodians to help me break it down, creating another headache. Morris Muzicale, the director of the Bigtime Symphony Orchestra, hated it when I broke something in his auditorium.

Olivia stepped into the hallway, fiddling with her engagement ring. Octavia hurried to her sister's side, and I was immediately forgotten, as usual.

I checked my watch again. Four minutes, three seconds.

I looked over at Paul. "Are you ready? It's almost time."

Paul continued to slump in the chair, staring at nothing in particular. I had to repeat myself, putting more bite into my words, before he looked at me, sighed, and heaved himself to his feet.

Octavia kissed her sister's cheek, smoothed back Olivia's hair, and murmured into her ear. "What were you thinking? Pull yourself together. *Right now.*"

Though she spoke in a harsh whisper, I heard Octavia loud and clear, thanks to my superhearing.

"It will all be over soon," Octavia continued, "and you can go back to your incessant shopping and partying and pretend like everything is fine."

Olivia dropped her gaze and didn't look at Octavia.

Those weren't the kindest or most reassuring words to say to your sister, but who was I to judge? I'd learned a long time ago that spouting sunshine rarely got the job done. This wasn't the first dysfunctional family dynamic I'd seen, and it wouldn't be the last. This whole incident was rather tame in comparison to some of the things I'd witnessed. Bitch slaps, hair pulling, stabbings, the occasional shooting. I even had one bride take a hot curling iron to her mother's face because she found mommy dearest screwing her intended. Yeah, the O'Haras ranked pretty low on the Richter scale when it came to family feuds.

Octavia patted Olivia's cheek and stepped aside so Paul could squeeze into the picture. He offered Olivia his arm. She gave him an uncertain smile and took it, her brown eyes a bit glassy. Olivia was feeling no pain now. Ah, relaxidon, the anti-anxiety wonder drug.

I pulled my cell phone out from another pocket on my vest. Thanks to the video cameras I'd hooked up earlier, the phone screen showed me the inside of the auditorium. Flowers, decorations, and five hundred invited guests crowded into the space. In addition to hosting an engagement party for her sister, Octavia intended to announce Oomph's buyout of Polish, the lip-care company Paul's family owned. This was definitely a *merger* in every sense of the word.

I hit a button on the phone, and the screen flicked to another camera. The band members were clustered together at the foot of the stage, having just finished a number and preparing to play the entrance music. The guests had turned toward the doors, waiting on Olivia and Paul. I checked my watch. Fifty-seven seconds.

I activated the headset clamped to the side of my head. "Talk to me, Chloe."

"We're a go," Chloe Cavanaugh, my right-hand woman, chirped in my ear. "The band's ready, and everyone's eager to get a glimpse of the happy couple."

I glanced at the screen once more. The house lights dimmed, until only candles flickered in the auditorium. As I watched, a spotlight appeared on the doors where Olivia and Paul would make their grand appearance.

Satisfied everything was as perfect as it was going to get, I signaled to the two waiting ushers to open the doors.

"All right," I told Chloe. "Here they come."

Olivia gave me another soft, dreamy look before she and Paul stepped inside. Gasps, claps, and murmurs of appreciation swept through the crowd.

I nodded. Another job well done—so far.

Olivia and Paul moved through the throngs of guests with Octavia watching their every step. I headed for the concrete stairs leading to the second-floor, balcony level of the auditorium.

I emerged onto the landing, and Chloe turned at the sound of my footsteps. Chloe was a petite woman in her late twenties with black hair, hazel eyes, and olive skin. Like me, she wore a simple black pantsuit. Unlike me, she didn't have a vest on over the top of it.

I'd offered to buy Chloe a vest when I'd hired her six months ago, but she'd politely refused. She thought she could get by with what she had stuffed in her pint-sized purse. Rookie. Chloe hadn't been through the disasters I had. She'd learn, though—if she lasted that long. Most of my employees tended to burn out after a few months. They couldn't handle the pressure I put on them—or myself.

"How is everything?" I asked, moving to stand beside her.

Chloe swept out her hand. "See for yourself."

I peered over the metal railing to the floor below. Earlier today, workers had removed the auditorium seats and had them replaced with thick, padded benches. Balloons shaped like enormous red lips, Oomph's logo, bobbed up and down at the ends of the benches, while faux ivory columns ringed the area. The columns held up a sheer silk netting embossed with more lips and filled with red roses, ivy, and baby's breath. Lights entwined with the roses made the velvet petals glow. I'd been worried about the heat from the lights igniting the flowers, but everything seemed to be okay—for now.

Olivia and Paul made their way to the middle of the

auditorium, where they shook hands and kissed cheeks. If the relaxidon didn't take Olivia's mind off her worries, maybe the constant attention would. She'd barely have time to breathe for the next thirty minutes.

From this distance, Olivia and Paul resembled two delicate figures on top of a wedding cake, surrounded by an army of moving, glittering frosting. At least, they would have to most people. I could see them as clearly as if they stood right in front of me. I might not care for some of my supersenses, but the enhanced eyesight was a perk—most of the time.

Chloe shook her head. "You've done it again, Abby. I can't believe you planned this party on a week's notice. It looks like it took months."

I couldn't believe it either. I might be *the* professional event planner in Bigtime, but even I had difficulty throwing together a high-society soiree in five business days. But Octavia had insisted. Her baby sister's engagement and the Oomph and Polish merger had to be announced simultaneously by mid-January in the most lavish manner possible. Olivia freaking out right before the party had been the least of my problems. Given the time crunch, I'd had to beg, badger, and berate everyone from the caterers to the florist to the band. Well, more so than usual. But somehow, it had all come together at the last minute.

My critical gaze moved from one thing to another. Decorations. Flowers. Lip balloons. Olivia. Paul.

A sense of accomplishment, of pride, filled me. I might sometimes hate parties and the crises that went along with them, but nothing satisfied me more than a job well done. Chloe was right. Everything was perfect. Just the way it should be.

Just the way I'd planned.

CHAPTER TWO

The engagement party kicked into full swing. Olivia and Paul kept smiling and shaking hands while the band played jazzy music. The guests sipped champagne as they waited their turn in the receiving line.

But my job wasn't done yet. In addition to wanting her sister to announce her engagement in the richest manner possible, Octavia had demanded the accompanying sit-down dinner—focusing on the merger of the two companies—be just as marvelous, which meant more work for me.

"You stay here and supervise," I said. "I'm going to the dining hall to make sure everything's set up there."

Chloe nodded.

I moved down the stairs to the ground floor of the convention center, stopping a moment to twist my neck from side to side. I was rewarded with a slight *pop* as my tension-filled bones found a bit of relief. January usually was one of my slowest months, but this one had been nonstop action. I'd done five weddings in as many weeks. With Valentine's Day only a month away, I was already hip deep into planning couples' dinners and romantic rendezvous. On the big day, I wouldn't have a moment to myself—I'd be too busy overseeing everyone else's happiness.

Did I mention I hate some holidays too?

I checked my watch. The two-inch-wide silver timepiece was more like a small computer. It boasted three separate black faces, each one showing the minutes and seconds remaining until the next events were supposed to start. Four minutes, twenty-nine seconds before the dining hall doors opened. Fifteen minutes before the food would be set out. Thirty minutes until Olivia, Paul, and the rest of the guests entered the dining room.

Satisfied everything was on schedule, I set off down the corridor.

The Bigtime Convention Center had more square footage than almost any other building in the city. I'd planned and overseen so many weddings, parties, and fundraisers here I knew the layout blindfolded. I used my master key to open a door marked *Staff Only* and entered another hallway.

The twisting corridor was the belly of the beast. It ran the length of the center, a secret passage offering access to every part of the building. At first, the dimly lit hallway with its faceless concrete walls had creeped me out, but I'd gotten used to it. I couldn't afford not to.

More than once, I'd stashed some drunken best man down here so he could sleep off his buzz rather than tell his buddy the groom that he was secretly in love with the bride. Sometimes, I thought I should give up event planning and just start blackmailing people. I had enough dirt to bury several of Bigtime's high rollers.

I closed the door behind me, stepped onto a strip of gray carpet, and walked on. The concrete floor used to be as bare as the walls, and you could hear someone's footsteps ring out the entire length of the hallway. Since my karaoke accident and subsequent acquisition of supersenses, loud, sharp noises aggravated me—and echoing footsteps almost always guaranteed a killer migraine. So, I'd convinced Morris Muzicale to put some carpet down here, along with a couple of cots, blankets, and pillows for my under-the-table party guests. I'd also brought in my own supplies—bottled water, protein bars, relaxidon, and a spare vest, all of which were stashed in my locker. Now, the convention center was like a second home.

I reached a door marked *Dining Hall 5*, used my key to unlock it, and stepped through. A six-foot-high potted palm tree partially obscured the entrance. I shut the door behind me and wiggled past the green leaves.

The dining hall looked similar to the auditorium, with its netting of roses and lights. But instead of benches, round tables large enough to seat eight people each ringed a parquet dance floor. A projector screen hung down one wall behind a podium flanked by two long tables. The happy couple and miscellaneous family members would sit there, and Octavia would announce the merger from the podium later. More Oomph lip balloons were tied to various columns. A banner stretched across the front of the podium read *Olivia + Paul, Oomph + Polish = Two Matches Made in Heaven.*

Lip-shaped crystal bowls sat on every table, each filled with samples of Oomph cosmetics. The guests would take the samples with them, instead of more traditional party favors.

Waiters bustled around the dining hall, lighting the candles on the tables and popping the corks off champagne bottles. One of the waiters stepped through a door leading to the kitchen. With my supersense of smell, it was easy to distinguish among the various aromas. Red-pepper-crusted chicken, garlic mashed potatoes, Parmesan-dusted asparagus, warm pumpernickel bread.

Olivia and Paul had forgone the typical bland dinner fare of baked chicken and fish in favor of more unusual dishes. Or rather, Octavia had. She'd insisted all of the food be red, white, black, or green—Oomph's corporate colors. It wasn't the strangest request I'd gotten. Nothing could top Milton Moore's desire for strippers wrestling in a pit of strawberry gelatin at his ninetieth birthday party. Still, I'd tried to point out how limiting color-coordinated food could be, but the customer was always right—and Octavia always got what she wanted. Besides, she was paying me enough to do whatever she wanted, whenever she wanted—short of sleeping with her. Even then, I might consider it.

But right now, I had a caterer to talk to.

"Where's Kyle?" I asked one of the waitresses.

She jerked her thumb over her shoulder in the direction of the kitchen. I pushed through the swinging double doors. A dozen chefs wearing food-spattered aprons and tall, white hats crammed inside, chopping vegetables and yelling out instructions. More waiters scooped and arranged mounds of potatoes and pounds of chicken onto plates. Kyle Quicke stood in the middle of it all.

A tall guy with a very lean figure, blue eyes, and a mop of sandy hair, Kyle owned Quicke's, his family's restaurant. Thanks to some secret recipes, Quicke's served up the best food in the city. Everybody loved it, and it was my go-to restaurant for catering events. Kyle hadn't blinked an eye when I'd told him I needed five hundred pounds of chicken in less than a week. It took a lot to ruffle Kyle, who took everything in stride.

"Abby Appleby." Kyle smiled. "I was wondering when you were going to show up. Are you okay? You look a little tired."

I was tired. I'd been working eighteen-hour days for the past week to make sure this party went off without a hitch, but I wasn't about to tell him. If there was one thing an event planner could never do, it was show weakness. People expected you to be cool, calm, and in control—and more or less awake—always.

"Well, here I am. You know what I was wondering, Kyle? Where my lip-shaped cake is. It's supposed to be outside when the guests come into the dining hall. A big visual reminder of the merger. We talked and talked and *talked* about this."

Actually, I'd done most of the talking. With a touch of berating. Maybe it was the perfectionist in me, but I tended to get a little worked up at my events. All right, a lot worked up. Most of the time, I was able to get things done just by politely asking, but the rougher the going, the louder my voice got. My customers paid me to deliver the best, to make sure every detail was seen to, no matter how small, trivial, and inconsequential. Perfection was what I'd built my business, my reputation, on, and I liked to deliver. Molding chaos into birthdays, parties, and weddings to remember gave me a sense of accomplishment, satisfaction, and pride.

I pointed to a table where the cakes sat—five of them, courtesy of Bryn's Bakery. Four chocolate layer cakes, and one monstrous, red, liplike behemoth with seven butter cream-filled layers. I thought the giant lips looked a little garish and creepy, but that wouldn't stop Bigtime's finest from digging into the cake—provided it made it outside on time.

"Abby?" Chloe's voice crackled in my ear. "A few folks are leaving the auditorium, and Olivia and Paul have just started posing for the photos. Everyone should be headed your way in about ten minutes."

"Thanks, Chloe."

I turned back to Kyle, but he'd already moved to the other side of the kitchen, despite the fact that his chefs blocked the aisles. Kyle was stealthy. He always managed to slip out of reach whenever my back was turned. He has excellent survival instincts.

"I know, I know, get the cakes out pronto, or you'll have my guts for garters," Kyle said, still smiling. "Relax, Abby. You worry too much."

I really must be tired, because I was getting a little too predictable. I'd have to come up with some new threats for Kyle Quicke.

Kyle and the waiters placed the cakes on the dining hall tables a scant twenty-seven seconds before people started filing inside. Everyone made a beeline for the desserts, just as I'd predicted. By the time Olivia and Paul arrived, the first round of food and drinks had been served, and guests had consumed three of the chocolate cakes.

Waiters brought in the chicken entrées, and everyone drifted away to their tables to eat. I stationed Chloe behind a column next to the stage so she could see to the needs of Olivia, Paul, and their family members while I took up a position next to the kitchen to make sure the food and drinks kept coming.

Nothing much happened during dinner, and finally, Octavia got up to toast her sister and soon-to-be brother-in-law—and announce the merger of their companies.

"This is not only a joining together of two terrific people but of two visionary businesses," Octavia said.

A spotlight fell on Olivia and Paul. Maybe it was just the glare, but the two of them weren't exactly smiling—more like cringing.

"With Oomph's recent acquisition of Polish, we will continue to bring you not only the finest makeup but also the best lip-care products on the market," Octavia continued.

She raised her champagne glass, and everyone applauded. Octavia's speech soon drifted into the land of stock speak, the way these things always did. I tuned most of it out.

A few minor crises occurred during the evening, most notably Paul's father, Peter Potter, getting drunk and trying to wrest the microphone away from Octavia. But I muscled Peter into the bathroom, shoved his head under the sink, and got him sobered up enough to return to the party.

At least no superheroes or ubervillains decided to crash the dinner. I worried about that with every event. A villain might decide to hold everyone hostage—or worse, take all of the food and booze with her. The fear was greater now, since a museum benefit I'd recently helped to plan had ended in disaster just that way—not once, but twice—with Berkley Brighton, the richest man in the city, getting killed in the crossfire.

Speaking of rich people, more than a few were in attendance tonight. The O'Hara-Potter engagement and merger were big news, as both families were worth a couple hundred million. Sam Sloane, Devlin Dash, Wesley Weston, Grace Caleb, and dozens of other business tycoons populated the room. The society and other reporters for the newspapers and TV stations had also come out to cover the event, including Carmen Cole with *The Exposé* and Kelly Caleb of the Superhero News Network.

I spotted Joanne James in the crowd, talking with Bella Bulluci. Joanne was hard to miss with her mane of black curls, lithe body, and sharp tongue. Bella, meanwhile, was a quiet, curvy, petite woman with frizzy hair. The two couldn't have been more different, but they'd recently become good friends.

Joanne and Bella had been at the museum benefit the second time ubervillains had struck, and they'd both been kidnapped. Although they'd survived, Joanne's husband, Berkley, had been killed. I'd planned his funeral a few months ago. It was one of the hardest jobs I'd ever done, mainly because I had only a couple of days to pull together what amounted to a state funeral.

But Joanne had seemed pleased with my efforts, enough to hire me to coordinate some of the other events accompanying Berkley's passing, including all of the dedications and ribbon-cuttings his benefactors were holding. The whiskey mogul had been worth billions, and he'd spread his wealth to dozens of

Bigtime charities. Pretty soon, Berkley Brighton's name would be on just about every building in the city.

I waved to Joanne and Bella, trying to catch their attention, but the two women were deep in conversation—one I could hear, despite the ambient noise in the room.

"I still can't believe Jasper is your brother," Bella said, "and that the two of you don't speak."

"Are you on that again?" Joanne snapped. "I told you Jasper and I don't have the same cozy relationship you have with your brother, Johnny. We never have."

"I'm just worried about you. That's what friends do. They worry about each other."

Joanne rolled her eyes, but she linked her arm through the younger woman's. "There you go again, being all sugary sweet and concerned and making my teeth hurt. Don't worry, Bella. I'm fine. Or as fine as I can be with Berkley gone."

The two women started talking about other things, including Bella's significant other, Devlin Dash. I waved again, but Joanne and Bella didn't see me, didn't even look in my direction, didn't even know I was alive. Nobody saw me at events. I faded into the background, just like the Invisible Ingénues did. Oh, people knew I was around, but they didn't actually *look* for me—unless they needed something. In addition to having supersenses, I was an invisible woman—whether I wanted to be or not.

So, I quit listening to Bella and Joanne and went back to work. I stood against the wall, eyes flicking around, ears open wide, using my superpowers to make sure every single thing was still perfect.

By the time we got through the toasts, dinner, and dancing, it was almost midnight. I shifted on my aching feet. I would have loved to leave hours ago, but I always stayed until the bitter end. The one time I'd left a wedding before the reception ended, the maid of honor had tossed champagne on one of the groomsmen just as the waiter served the baked Alaska. One thing had led to another, until the Bigtime Fire Department had to be called out to save what was left of the church. So, I didn't take any chances now.

"Oh, Abby?"

I jumped at the sound of Octavia's voice. She stood beside me, propping up a very drunk Peter Potter. Superhearing or not, I'd been so preoccupied I hadn't even heard them approach. Good thing I wasn't a superhero and they weren't ubervillains. I might have been in serious trouble then.

"Yes, Octavia?"

She murmured in my ear. "I'm afraid Peter still isn't...feeling well. Do you think you could take him someplace and get him to lie down for a while?"

In other words, could I stash the embarrassing relative out of the way so everybody else could keep having a good time. I might call myself a professional event planner, but I was really just a glorified shrink, pharmacist, and babysitter rolled into one.

Before I could respond, Peter's stomach rumbled. His round face paled, and I could hear his rapid heartbeat and ragged breathing even over the music. All the signs of a man about to be violently sick.

I stepped back but wasn't quite quick enough. I doubted even the superhero Swifte would have been with his superspeed. Peter lurched forward, bent over, and puked all over me. The hot, sour stench of booze hit my nose while warm, squishy things I didn't want to think about splattered onto my shoes and pants.

Oh, yes. I *definitely* hated engagement parties.

CHAPTER THREE

Thankfully, only a few stragglers saw Peter upchuck all over my shoes. I fished a ginger tablet out of my vest and gave it to the businessman to help his queasy stomach. By the time I put him in a limo home, went to the bathroom, and cleaned myself up, everyone else had left.

I walked back to the dining hall to find it deserted. Thanks to the convention center's staff and Kyle and his army of workers, the decorations and dirty dishes had already been cleared away. The area had been returned to its usual, empty, pristine shell, just as Kyle had agreed to in the contract. I might not care for his lackadaisical attitude, but Kyle always was efficient.

Because everything had been taken care of, I trudged back to the hidden corridor and made my way to the staff break room. A couple of vending machines hunkered inside the windowless area, flanked by several plastic tables and rows of metal lockers. A man wearing gray janitor's coveralls sat at one of the tables, drinking a soda and chain smoking while he flipped through a hunting magazine.

"Hey, Colt," I said, moving to my locker and spinning the combination lock.

"Hey, Abby. How was the party?" Colt Colton asked, taking another drag off his cigarette.

"Not too bad, except for the guy who puked on my shoes."

Colt leaned over and stared at my black pumps, which weren't quite so black anymore. "That's messed up, Abby."

"Tell me about it."

He started to reply, but his cell phone rang. He tapped the screen and started talking.

I threw my puked-upon shoes in the trash. Digging some wool socks and my snow boots out of the locker, I plopped down in one of the chairs and pulled them on. Colt finished his call, crushed out his cigarette, and swallowed the rest of his soda.

"Duty calls." He folded up the magazine and stuck it in his back pocket. "Later, Abby."

"Later, Colt."

The custodian left the break room. The second the door shut behind him, I reached into my locker, pulled out an industrial-sized can of air freshener, and sprayed a liberal amount. Cigarette smoke always aggravated my supersenses. It never failed to make my eyes itch, nose twitch, and skin crawl. Unfortunately, Colt had a two-pack-a-day habit, and the break room always reeked of smoke.

I put the air freshener back into the locker, grabbed my black coat, and shrugged into it. A black toboggan went on my head. I glanced at my watch. Just after one in the morning. I thought about calling Piper Perez, my best friend, to see if she wanted to get a drink, but it was too late to go to The Blues, the karaoke bar we still frequented despite my unfortunate accident there. So, I buttoned up my coat, pulled on my gloves, wrapped a scarf around my face and neck, and headed out.

The party guests had long deserted the convention center, leaving the long, wide hallways still and silent. Thick, crimson carpet stretched across the floor, while sheer, matching fabric covered the walls. Gold threads arranged in paisley patterns in the fabric shimmered under the low glow of the house lights. More gold glinted on the Renaissance-style paintings, while murky shadows sprawled across the floor and crept up the walls. I made a right and entered the lobby, with its hundred-foot-high ceiling, elegant chandeliers, and gold-leaf crown molding.

Eddie Edgars, the college-age guard who manned the front desk, waved at me, then returned to his reading. Even though I was about fifty feet away, I could see the cover. Eddie was engrossed in a comic book by Confidante that chronicled the latest adventures of the Fearless Five, Bigtime's most powerful and popular superhero team. Each of the members—Striker, Fiera, Mr. Sage, Hermit, and Karma Girl—was featured in a heroic pose on the cover. I waved back to Eddie, pushed through the revolving doors, and stepped outside.

A hard spurt of wind slapped me in the face, chilling my cheeks through my scarf. It had snowed while I was inside, and several inches blanketed the street. A cold front had been stalled over Bigtime for a week. Every day, it snowed a little more, adding to what was already on the ground. The forecasters were calling for an actual blizzard tonight.

I reached through a slit in my coat and turned on the pocket-sized heater hidden in my vest. The machine clicked on, and warm air rushed across my chest, fighting back the cold. Let Chloe scoff all she wanted. There were advantages to having a vest of many things.

I stuck my gloved hands in my pockets, tucked my chin down, and walked on. I'd recently moved to a loft in the city so I could be closer to my office. My building was only a few blocks from the convention center, but the snow made it slow going.

Quiet cloaked the streets, along with the snow. Only an occasional puff of wind whistled at the icy silence. I enjoyed the tranquility after the clang, clatter, and conversation of the party. I'd learned to tune out much of the noise that aggravates my enhanced hearing, but I still ended up with killer headaches after some of my more boisterous events. Tonight, I'd been lucky; I had only a dull ache in my temples.

I'd just passed an alley on Thirteenth Street when a strange noise broke the cold quiet. It sounded like a large zipper being drawn down. A soft sound, no louder than a whisper, I wouldn't have heard it at all if everything else hadn't been so still.

I continued on my way, but when I heard a different noise, like metal scraping together, I stopped and concentrated, trying to find the source of the sounds. They seemed to be coming from deeper in the alley. I stepped inside a shadow at the far end and reached for my stun gun.

The alley ran about a hundred feet straight back before curving to the right. A few Dumpsters sat against the brick walls, and shadows pooled around them like blood. I looked—*really* looked—toward the end of the alley where the shadows were the darkest. Most people would have seen nothing but blackness ringed with snow, but I wasn't most people. Not anymore. My vision was just as good at night as it was during the day.

The sound of metal clanged together again. A black zip line uncoiled at the end of the alley, and a figure slid to a stop, his booted feet crunching into the snow-covered ground.

His back was to me as he undid a buckle securing him to the line. He held up something that resembled a gun and pressed a button. The line, which had a silver hook attached to the end, zipped into the gun, like a tape measure being drawn into its case, and he stuck the weapon in a leg holster. He turned then, and I got a look at the noisemaker.

He wore a cobalt-blue leather costume that outlined his muscular body. In a darker shade of blue, a fierce-looking bird with outstretched wings spread across his chest. But the most prominent parts of the bird were its talons, which appeared ready to erupt from the costume and slice you with their sharp, curved edges. A harness around the man's right thigh held a gun topped by what looked like a small crossbow, while the one on his left leg contained the gun with the grappling hook I'd just seen him use. A belt studded with crossbow bolts encircled his lean waist. A cobalt toboggan covered his hair, probably to protect him from the cold, while a wide, blue-tinted, wing-shaped visor wrapped around his face, obscuring most of it from sight.

It was Talon, one of Bigtime's many superheroes. Talon was a bit of a Robin Hood. He frequently robbed the rich to give to charity. At least, he robbed the rich drug dealers and gangsters who populated the city. Unfortunately, there were almost as many of those as there were ubervillains.

Talon also wasn't your typical hero in one other respect—he didn't have a superpower. At least, none I knew of. Most of your Bigtime heroes and villains fell into one of two categories. They were either Ps or Gs—powers or gadgets. That was how I thought of them. Superheroes like Fiera, the member of the Fearless Five who could form fireballs with her bare hands, were Ps. Heroes like Talon, who relied on complicated weapons and other gizmos, were Gs. I admired the Gs much more than the Ps. Anyone with a power could be a hero. It took someone with a lot of guts to be a hero without any superpowers.

There was a finesse to Talon's gizmos, a cool cleverness I appreciated far more than the brute strength some of the other heroes used to fight evil. The crossbow-topped gun on his thigh could do everything from shoot darts to morph into a quarterstaff, and his grappling hook gun had a myriad of functions as well. At least, that was what my friend Piper said. She knew everything there was to know about Bigtime's superheroes and ubervillains.

Talon slid something small, skinny, and silver into a slot on his belt. I shrugged and turned, ready to get to my warm, cozy loft, when another odd sound caught my ear. It sounded like more zippers—a lot more zippers.

A second later, six men dressed in dark clothes rappelled down into the alley.

"There he is!"

"Get him!"

"Don't let him get away!"

Talon whirled to face the men as they ganged up on him, but he more than held his own. In addition to being a gadget guru, he was a solid street fighter. The superhero punched, kicked, and took down one man after another. I just stood there and watched, too awestruck to do anything else.

Talon had just dispatched the last man when a gun burped orange fire from the other side of the alley. A bullet pierced Talon's left shoulder, and he cried out in pain. Clutching his shoulder, he stumbled back. The bullet kept going. It hit the wall behind him and exploded, spewing a black gas in Talon's face. The superhero screamed, as though the gas burned him. I shrank back against the alley wall.

A figure eased out of the shadows where the bullet had come from. He looked like a bad guy from some old spaghetti western movie. He wore a long, black leather duster and cowboy boots, complete with silver tips and jangling silver spurs. Black hair hung loose to his shoulders, while a black-and-white, paisley bandana covered the bottom half of his face. A black, ten-gallon hat was pushed low on his forehead. He held a silver revolver, except it was much larger than your typical gun. I knew who he was too—Bandit, one of the city's ubervillains who was known for his two six-shooters. The handguns fired a variety of unusual projectiles, in addition to bullets. Bandit was a gun for hire, so to speak, an ubervillain who pimped himself out as a mercenary and enforcer to anyone who could pay his price.

Gun drawn, Bandit moved in front of Talon, who slumped against the alley wall, clutching his wounded shoulder. The other men limped to their feet, forming a semicircle around the injured superhero.

"Tycoon wants what you took from him," Bandit said, drawling out each and every syllable. "Now."

Tycoon was mixed up in this too? A whole smorgasbord of heroes and villains had come out to play tonight. Tycoon was Bigtime's most notorious mob boss—and one of the most secretive. He'd never been photographed, and only two or three of his most trusted lieutenants even knew what he looked like or who he really was. More info gleaned from Piper. She paid attention to such things.

Tycoon could have been an ubervillain for all his secrecy. Yet somehow, he managed to run an empire of gambling and prostitution—and never get caught. Lately, the rumor mill and news outlets buzzed about him branching out and dealing in euphoridon, a very dangerous, very addictive radioactive drug with all sorts of nasty side effects.

"Tycoon...can go...to hell," Talon said. "And you with him."

Bandit raised his gun and leveled it at Talon's heart. "Fine. Dead bodies are always easier to search anyway."

I couldn't believe what I was seeing. Talon with a bullet wound in his shoulder—and about to be killed by an ubervillain. I might know a thing or two about handling drunken businessmen, anxious debutantes, and carefree caterers, but this was beyond my area of expertise. By the time I called the police, Talon would be dead, and Bandit would have whatever he was after.

I decided to improvise, something I was pretty good at. Through the slits in my coat, I patted the various pockets of my vest, searching for something useful. I'd once saved the mayor from embarrassment by spray-painting red polka dots all over her white suit after she'd sat down in a puddle of ketchup at a restaurant opening. Surely, I had something that could help save a superhero. Gum, breath mints, tissues, hairspray, more relaxidon pills...

My fingers closed over my cell phone. I whipped it out and turned it around, shielding the screen's light from the goons in the alley. They probably couldn't see me anyway, but I didn't want to take any chances.

I tore off my glove and scrolled through the various ring tones until I came to the one I needed—the police siren. I'd used it before to sober up wasted frat boys and sorority girls at college mixers.

I called up the sound file and pressed *Play*. Half a dozen sirens erupted from the phone. It didn't sound like the real deal to my supersensitive ears, but it should be good enough to fool Bandit and his gang of thugs. At least, I hoped it was. Otherwise, there would be one less superhero in Bigtime.

Bandit's head whipped around to the end of the alley where I stood. I forced myself not to shrink back into the shadows. I didn't think he could see me, because I wore black from head to toe, but I wasn't going to draw attention to myself by moving. You never knew what ubervillains would do—or what they were capable of.

"Bandit! Let's get out of here!" one of the men said. "The cops are coming!"

I cranked up the volume, trying to add to the illusion.

Bandit kept staring in my direction, probably looking for the red and blue flash of the oncoming police cars. A small *click* rang out above the roar of my cell phone. Somehow, during the commotion, Talon had managed to straighten up—and he now had his crossbow gun pointed at Bandit's back.

The ubervillain looked over his shoulder, then back in my direction. I turned up the volume on the phone as loud as it would go, hoping it would be enough to save Talon.

"This isn't over, Talon," Bandit snarled. "Tycoon wants you dead. We'll be back for what you took."

Bandit spat on the snow, swiveled on his booted heel, and stomped through the right side of the alley. The other men limped along behind him. Talon held on until they left. Then, he let out a low groan and fell to one knee. Blood dripped from the wound on his shoulder, staining the white powder a harsh crimson.

I waited to be sure Bandit and his men weren't coming back before I scurried to the end of the alley. "Are you all right?"

Talon paid no attention to me. Instead, he clawed off his visor and scooped handfuls of snow onto his eyes. The superhero had his back to me, so I couldn't see his face.

"It burns," he said to no one in particular. "Damn, that burns."

I assumed he was talking about the gas that had erupted from the bullet Bandit had shot him with. My foot snagged on something in the snow, and I grunted and yanked it free. Talon froze. Then, he sprang into action, searching the ground around him. His fingers closed over his visor, and he slipped it on his face before turning toward me.

"Is someone there?" he asked.

I opened my mouth to respond when I realized Talon wasn't looking in my direction. I was less than six feet away, but his head was pointed off to the right, as if I was standing over there. But there was no way he could have avoided seeing me. Even I wasn't that invisible.

Unless...he *couldn't* see me.

Maybe he couldn't. The gas must have penetrated his visor, gotten into his eyes, and blinded him. I wondered if the effect was temporary—or permanent.

"Is someone there?" Talon repeated, moving into a low crouch, his hand tightening on his crossbow gun.

I could tell by the sharpness in his voice that he was worried I'd seen him—that I knew who he was. I didn't know what to do, so I played dumb. I waited a beat, then scuffled around in the snow as if I'd just arrived.

"What happened?" I asked, playing the part of the upstanding citizen.

Talon gestured at the blood trickling down his shoulder. "I got shot."

I started to open my mouth to respond but thought better of it. From the way I was stating the obvious, you would have thought I was the one who was blind.

"That. Right. Let me call the police."

He frowned. "They're almost here, aren't they?"

I looked down and realized my phone was still on and still blaring out the sound of sirens.

"Oh no," I said, shutting it off. "That's just one of my cell phone ring tones. I heard a strange noise and clicked it on. It's something I do whenever I'm nervous."

Talon cocked his head to one side as if I was spouting nonsense. Maybe I was. So much had happened in the past few minutes. It was a lot to process.

"But you're hurt. Let me call the cops for real. They'll bring an ambulance and take you to the hospital—"

"No!" he said. "No cops, no ambulance, no hospital. I'll be all right. Just give me a minute."

"All right? You have a bullet wound in your shoulder. How is that *all right*?"

The wet, coppery stench of his blood made my stomach twist. That was the bad thing about having supersenses—I heard and felt and smelled bad things that much *more*. These days, being exposed to even a bit of blood was more than enough to make me light-headed.

Talon reached out and fumbled at my hand, the one holding the phone. His fingers closed around my wrist. Good grief, the man had a strong grip, even though he'd just been shot.

"I can't just leave you out here," I said. "You're bleeding, and it's snowing again. You'll get hypothermia in no time."

His fingers tightened on my wrist. The palm of his hand was rough and cold, his fingers hard and calloused, but a hot tingle traveled up my arm at his touch. A small rush of interest, of attraction, I hadn't felt in a long time. I wasn't into superheroes, not like Piper, who could recite obscure facts about every hero and villain in town, but I found myself very curious and very drawn to Talon.

"No. Promise me you won't call the police. They can't protect me. Bandit will come to the hospital and finish the job, and I won't be able to stop him. Not now. And a lot of innocent people could get hurt if they get in his way."

"But—" I protested.

"No, no police."

I drew in a breath and opened my mouth to argue when I caught a whiff of his scent. He smelled like snow mixed with mint—crisp, cold, sharp, clean. A wonderful aroma, even if it was tinged with blood.

I looked up into his face. I couldn't see his eyes, of course. The blue, wraparound visor hid them from view, but he had a strong, square jaw. Talon wasn't really handsome, not like Debonair or one of the other suave superheroes, but he had a rugged look that appealed to me.

He was Talon. A superhero. A larger-than-life G-man who went around the city making things right.

And I found myself nodding in total agreement, as if it was a perfectly reasonable plan, instead of the dumbest thing I'd ever heard.

"All right. I won't call the cops."

"Good." Talon smiled. "And let me thank you. If it wasn't for you, I wouldn't be breathing at the moment. Now, can I ask you to do one more thing for me?"

"Anything," I asked, mesmerized.

"Help me stand up."

I scooted closer to him and put my shoulder under his left arm. He was heavier than I expected—much heavier than Peter Potter had been. Then again, Talon was all leather-clad muscle, whereas Peter had been all portly businessman. I made sure my boots were steady beneath me, then rose to my feet. I'm sure there were some women in Bigtime who would have gracefully guided Talon to his feet, who would have been strong and solid while still maintaining elegance and girly-girl mystique. Not me. I grunted like a noisy tennis player from the effort of hauling the superhero upright.

But I managed it, and we stood there, like lovers in a heated clinch, my face pressed against his chin. A bit of dark stubble scraped against my skin, and I breathed in, enjoying his crisp, cold scent. Talon was a couple of inches over six feet but seemed larger, stronger in the dark night. I'd never paid much attention to superheroes, but I was definitely intrigued by the man before me. Even if he was bleeding all over my coat. Good thing it was black. At least I couldn't see the stains easily, even if I could smell them.

Talon slid his arm off my shoulder and took a step back. His boots skidded on the snow a moment before he found his footing.

"Are you sure you're okay?" I asked, still worried.

Talon's face was pale, despite the stubble darkening his chin. Beads of cold sweat glistened on his forehead, and his breath puffed out in ragged gasps—all signs of someone about to pass out, superhero or not.

"I'm fine," he said. "It's just a flesh wound. Now, I'm sure you want to get in out of the cold. So, it's time for me to go."

Talon grabbed at his leg harness, fumbling around until he found his grappling hook gun. Finally pulling it free, he raised it over his head and squeezed the trigger. The hook arced up into the night sky before clanging onto the roof above our heads. Talon clipped himself to the line and gave it a tug to make sure it was anchored on something solid.

"Thanks again for the rescue," Talon said, looking off to the left instead of at me. "Tonight, you're my hero."

Talon started to press a button on the side of the grappling hook gun, but his finger slipped off the gadget. He tried again, with the same result. The third time, he dropped the gun entirely. The superhero teetered from side to side, his legs crumpled, and he pitched forward, face-first into the snow.

I stared at his unconscious form. Snow drifted down from the black, winter sky, covering his cobalt-blue costume one white, crystal flake at a time.

I rubbed my aching head. I had a wounded, unconscious superhero who'd made me promise not to call the police and not take him to the hospital. Bandit and his thugs could come back any second, and the weather was going from bad to worse.

I was used to dealing with crises, but this was a doozy even for me.

What was I going to do now?

ABOUT THE AUTHOR

Jennifer Estep is a *New York Times*, *USA Today*, and international bestselling author, prowling the streets of her imagination in search of her next fantasy idea.

Jennifer is the author of the **Elemental Assassin** urban fantasy series. The books focus on Gin Blanco, an assassin codenamed the Spider who can control the elements of Ice and Stone. When she's not busy battling bad guys and righting wrongs, Gin runs a barbecue restaurant called the Pork Pit in the fictional Southern metropolis of Ashland. The city is also home to giants, dwarves, vampires, and elementals—Air, Fire, Ice, and Stone.

Jennifer is also the author of the **Mythos Academy** young adult urban fantasy series. The books focus on Gwen Frost, a 17-year-old girl who has the gift of psychometry, or the ability to know an object's history just by touching it. After a serious freak-out with her magic, Gwen is shipped off to Mythos Academy, a school for the descendants of ancient warriors like Spartans, Valkyries, Amazons, and more.

Jennifer is also the author of the **Black Blade** young adult urban fantasy series. The books focus on Lila Merriweather, a 17-year-old thief who lives in Cloudburst Falls, West Virginia, a town dubbed "the most magical place in America." Lila does her best to stay off the grid and avoid the Families—or mobs—who control much of the town. But when she saves a member of the

Sinclair Family during an attack, Lila finds herself caught in the middle of a brewing war between the Sinclairs and the Draconis, the two most powerful Families in town.

Jennifer is also the author of the **Bigtime** paranormal romance series. The books feature sexy superheroes, evil ubervillains, and smart, sassy gals.

For more information on Jennifer and her books, visit her website at www.JenniferEstep.com. You can also follow her on Facebook, Goodreads, and Twitter—@Jennifer_Estep.

Happy reading, everyone!

OTHER BOOKS
BY JENNIFER ESTEP

The Mythos Academy series

Books

Touch of Frost
Kiss of Frost
Dark Frost
Crimson Frost
Midnight Frost
Killer Frost

E-novellas and short stories

First Frost
Halloween Frost
Spartan Frost

The Black Blade series

Cold Burn of Magic
Dark Heart of Magic
Bright Blaze of Magic